BAD BOYS
AND THE GANGSTERS

Also in Beaver by Jim and Duncan Eldridge
How to Handle Grown-Ups
What Grown-Ups Say and What They Really Mean
Bogeys, Boils and Belly Buttons
More Ways to Handle Grown-Ups
Peregrine Peabody's Completely Misleading
History of the World
Bad Boyes

And by Jim Eldridge
The Wobbly Jelly Joke Book

BAD BOYES
AND THE GANGSTERS

Jim and Duncan Eldridge

Illustrated by David Mostyn

Beaver Books

A Beaver Book
Published by Arrow Books Limited
62–5 Chandos Place, London WC2N 4NW

An imprint of Century Hutchinson Ltd

London Melbourne Sydney Auckland
Johannesburg and agencies throughout the world

First published 1988

Set in Century Schoolbook
by JH Graphics Ltd, Reading

Made and printed in Great Britain
by Anchor Brendon Limited
Tiptree, Essex

ISBN 0 09 961020 5

Introduction

Hi, it's me again, Bryan Arthur Derek Boyes (as seen on television).

This is just to introduce you to this book and tell you it is wonderful and exciting and worth every penny you've paid for it. (If you're reading this in a bookshop, take it to the counter and pay for it immediately, otherwise the publishers won't give me any money.)

Who are the gangsters of the title, you are asking, and how did I get involved with them in the first place? Was it exciting and dangerous? The answer is . . . I can't tell you. If you want to find out exactly what happened, then turn over the page, and read on!

1

It was the icing on the cake that started it all.

(See, that's got you interested, hasn't it? It better had, otherwise I'm going to demand the money back that I paid for this book called *How To Write Best-Selling Books And Make Millions of Pounds.* According to it, if you begin with a short, punchy opening sentence, Hollywood producers turn up at your door in queues all holding fistfuls of money and offering to buy the film rights. Though, on second thoughts, a sentence about cake icing doesn't have all that much punch. Maybe I should have started with, 'The alien from Outer Space grabbed my mum with its long, spiny tentacles . . .' — but then you'd feel cheated because all I'd go on to talk about would be cake icing. So, back to the cake:)

I'd just walked in to our home after a hard day at school, dodging doing any work at all, and Mum had all this cooking stuff on the table, including a large cake. She'd obviously been about to spread a newspaper on the table to stop crumbs and sugar and stuff from getting all over the place, but had changed her mind and had started to read it instead. This meant that she didn't pay much attention to me as I walked in, and failed to notice that I was looking at the cake on the table in a hungry way. (A hard day's dodging at school gives you an appetite, believe me.) I decided to drop a subtle hint.

'Great!' I said. 'Cake! When can we eat it?'

'This isn't for eating,' said Mum; 'it's for exhibition.'

This threw me.

'Exhibiting a cake?' I said, baffled.

'The icing,' said Mum. She shook her head and gave a deep sigh. 'This is terrible!'

I looked at the cake.

'It doesn't look that bad,' I said, thinking that a bit of flattery wouldn't go amiss while there was still a chance of me getting my teeth into a bit of it.

'I'm not talking about the cake,' said Mum. 'I'm talking about this article in the paper. Did you know there's a huge illegal business operating locally, selling secrets?'

This sounded interesting.

'What, spying?' I asked.

'Of a sort. This is industrial espionage. Business secrets. They reckon that the centre of the trade is right here, right in this borough. Just think, there are Master Criminals operating in this area. Maybe in this very street!'

I gave a disparaging snort.

'I wouldn't think so,' I commented. 'Most of the people in this street are so dozy they couldn't even catch a cold, let alone be a Master Criminal.'

'Don't be rude,' said Mum, which is the usual reply my parents seem to give to most of my highly intelligent comments. Then she added, 'Actually, I'm glad you're home.'

This immediately made me suspicious. Normally my mother welcomes my arrival home in the same way as she'd welcome someone infected with the Bubonic Plague.

'Oh?' I said, guardedly.

'There's a book I need from the library. I'd get it myself but this icing is at a crucial stage.'

I flopped dramatically down on to the settee in my best state-of-exhaustion pose.

'I'm exhausted after a hard day at school,' I said.

'You can eat this cake after it's exhibited,' said Mum.

This was an offer that was worth investigating.

'What's the book called?' I asked.

'*Gothic Innovations in Egg-White Engineering Structures.*'

I frowned. It didn't sound like the best read under the sun.

'Is it a thriller?' I asked.

'No,' said Mum, with the sort of superior look she gives if anyone suggests that she might enjoy a good thriller or a Western or something. 'It's about cake icing. It's in the cookery section.'

And she turned back to whipping up some egg whites in a bowl. The whole thing was beginning to look very promising and tasty, so off I headed for the library.

And this is where we come to The Plot, as these professional writers call it.

If you remember, my mum had read something in the paper about a gang operating locally, selling industrial secrets. Now what I didn't know when I set off for the library was that this very same gang were operating not very far away from where I lived, and very shortly Our Paths Would Cross. (Good that, isn't it? Like a real thriller writer.)

Because I didn't know exactly what they were doing I will have to write about what they were up to from my imagination (in other words, make it up), and from the evidence that was given later by the police . . . but that's giving away the end of the book! So, to fill you in on what the crooks were doing while I was on my way to the library, and how we all would soon bump into each other, I will put in a row of dots, change to italic type and do the Creative Writing bit while we move the action of this book to a small room somewhere not far away from where I live.

● ● ● ● ● ● ● ● ● ● ●

It was a small room (not far away from where I live, in case you'd forgotten), and Bonnie and Clyde Hipp were studying a plan of the local library spread out on a table. Trying to look over them was their Heavy, a short man called Herbert, small on muscle and small on brain. (Great stuff, this, isn't it? I learnt how to write like this in Mrs Potter's Creative Writing lessons in Junior School.)

On the plan were two toy soldiers, which

Bonnie moved around to show Herbert what he had to do and where he had to go. She tapped one of the toy soldiers.

'This is Ruggles, the industrialist,' she said. 'He comes into the library, goes up to Herbert and gives him an envelope.' She looked at Herbert, fixing him with a grim stare, as if willing the instructions to imprint themselves on his brain. 'You make sure the money's all there. Then you give him the piece of paper with the name of the book written on it. Then he goes to the shelf, opens the book, takes the formula, and that's it. Right?'

Clyde beamed at her, and the ill-fitting wig on the top of his head gave a little dance as he nodded.

'Brilliant!' he said.

They both looked at Herbert, who stared blankly down at the plan on the table.

'Can we go through it once more?' he asked. 'I'm not completely sure of it.'

Clyde groaned in exasperation.

'We've already been through it six times!' he said.

Herbert shook his head.

'Five,' he said, holding up a hand with all the fingers outstretched. 'I've been counting.'

'It was six,' corrected Bonnie. 'You ran out of fingers.'

'Oh,' said Herbert, and he looked at his hand as if wondering whether he was a finger short. Clyde sighed wearily.

'Alright,' he said. 'Where do you want to go through it from?'

Herbert thought about it.

'From the bit where I came in here to find out what was going on,' he said.

Bonnie and Clyde exchanged looks.

'Excuse us one moment, Herbert,' said Bonnie.

She took Clyde by the arm and steered him away to a corner of the room out of earshot, leaving Herbert to play with the two toy soldiers, and so destroy the whole plan.

'Are you sure he's the right man for this job?' Bonnie asked in a low voice with a sideways look at Herbert.

Clyde shrugged helplessly.

'He's the only man,' he said.

Bonnie was not convinced.

'Are you telling me he's the only man who can do this job?' she demanded.

Clyde shook his head.

'No, I mean he's the only one available. All the rest of his gang got arrested robbing a bank.'

'How come he got away?' asked Bonnie, a faint hope dawning that she might have underestimated Herbert. That hope was quickly dashed.

'He turned up at the wrong bank,' said Clyde.

Bonnie frowned. 'I'm not sure about this . . .', she began.

'He'll be alright,' insisted Clyde. 'Otherwise it means one of us doing it and taking the chance of getting arrested.'

Bonnie thought this over.

'You're right,' she said.

They went back to the table and removed the two toy soldiers from Herbert's grasp.

'Right,' said Bonnie. 'Listen very carefully. I'll say it one more time.'

'Right,' said Herbert.

'We have got hold of a secret formula for making chips—'

Herbert frowned at her.

'Making chips?' he said. 'That's not very secret.'

'These chips,' said Clyde carefully, 'are made out of jelly.'

Herbert's frown increased even more, so much so it looked as if his face was going to fold in half.

'Won't they melt when you fry them?' he asked.

Bonnie and Clyde groaned in exasperation.

'Micro-chips!' they shouted.

'Oh,' said Herbert, as if in understanding. Then a thought crossed his mind. 'What flavour is the jelly?'

Very patiently, Clyde explained, while at the same time holding Bonnie off from attacking Herbert.

'This jelly,' he said, 'is made from electronic compounds systematically bound together in a radio-carbonated gelatin.'

'Oh,' said Herbert. He thought it over. 'Is that raspberry or strawberry flavour?'

'You don't eat this jelly!' snapped Bonnie impatiently. 'Now, a certain man will pay a lot of money for this formula.'

'A certain man,' said Herbert with a nod. 'Right.'

'Clyde is going to hide the formula in a book in the library,' continued Bonnie.

'Then I will leave the library,' said Clyde, taking up the plan. 'The man will come in—'

'The certain man,' said Herbert.

'Right,' said Clyde, pleased that Herbert was getting all this. 'It's a Mr Ruggles. He will give you an envelope. Inside that envelope will be money. You make sure the money is there, then you give him this piece of paper.'

Bonnie handed Herbert a piece of paper.

'That tells him which book the formula is hidden in.'

Herbert looked at the piece of paper.

'Say someone else takes the book first?' he asked.

Clyde gave a smug smile.

'They won't,' he said. 'Bonnie has chosen the most boring book she could find in that library to make sure that doesn't happen.'

'Gothic Innovations in Egg-White Engineering Structures,' said Bonnie proudly. 'Remember, it's in the cookery section.'

'Right,' said Herbert, the whole plot now firmly sunk into his brain. Then he frowned again. 'There's just one thing.'

'What's that?' asked Bonnie.

'Are you sure you couldn't eat this jelly with ice-cream?'

● ● ● ● ● ● ● ● ● ●

As I say, all this was going on completely unknown to me. In the meantime I was walking along the pavement on my way to the public library, doing a Good Deed, for which I hoped to get a good reward, when suddenly—

SCREEECH . . . !!

This huge car skidded to a halt with two wheels on the pavement, nearly running me over! I jumped back as the driver's door was thrown open. I expected the man who got out to rush over and ask me if I was alright, or at least to mumble a few apologetic noises. Instead of which he just pushed past me as if I wasn't even there and made straight for a telephone booth. Honestly! Not only was the man a dangerous driver, he was rude and ignorant to boot. I decided that anyone as obviously rotten as this deserved to be made to pay through the nose. After all, he could have killed me. I immediately put on a limp as I followed him.

'You nearly ran me over!' I said. 'I demand compensation.' Just to help him decide how much to pay me, I added helpfully, 'The last time I injured this leg I received a hundred pounds.'

His reaction was not at all what I'd expected. Instead of reaching into his pocket and handing me over a fiver to shut me up, he actually turned and pushed me away.

'Get out of my way!' he bellowed.

I stared after him open-mouthed as he went inside the phone booth.

'I'll settle for fifteen,' I called out.

He obviously wasn't a man used to making any concessions at all. He just went into the phone booth, picked up the phone and started dialling.

I stood there, glaring at his back for a moment. This man was a danger to all pedestrians everywhere, as well as to other road users. This man shouldn't be allowed on the roads.

I opened my school bag, which I still had with me, and pulled out a piece of unbreakable nylon string. I was going to show this road hog what happened to dangerous drivers who tried to run innocent children down and then acted without any sympathy. As I crept nearer the phone booth I could hear the man chattering away.

'Hello, Bonnie Hipp?' he was saying. 'This is Hector Ruggles. . . .Yes, I'm on my way to the library at the moment for the formula.'

Oh no you're not, I thought with a little smile, as I started to wrap the string round and round the telephone booth. Two circuits, and then I tied a double knot in the string, which meant that the crude and dangerous lunatic driver was safely tied inside the phone box. Once again, Bryan Boyes, Saviour of Pedestrians, had defeated an enemy of humanity!

I stepped back to admire my handiwork, just as this Ruggles character hung up the phone and went to open the door. At first he just thought the door was stuck and he pushed and pushed against it. Then he saw me, saw the string, and realized what had happened.

'Let me out, you rotten little rat!' he yelled. 'Untie this phone box or I'll—'

I decided not to wait around and find out what he intended to do to me if I didn't untie the phone box. After all, I am an impressionable child and bad language could very easily upset me and harm my development. So I blew a raspberry at him, and sauntered off towards the library.

Our local librarian, Miss Roberts, is a really funny old lady. (Adults keep telling me off for saying 'old' whenever I talk about her, but I can't see what they're complaining about. As far as I can tell she's nearly as old as my Granny, which puts her pretty much in the Ancient Fossil league, in my opinion.) Anyway, she gave a little jump of alarm when she saw me come into the library, a habit that I have noticed an awful lot of adults seem to have whenever they see me. I can only assume I produce some kind of allergic reaction in them.

'Yes?' said Miss Roberts, looking for somewhere to hide.

'My mum's sent me to collect a book,' I said. 'It's called *Gothic Innovations in Egg-White Engineering Structures.*'

At this I heard a sort of strangled 'Aargh' nearby.

I looked round. There was this little man standing near the shelves, goggling at me and flapping his arms to himself in a kind of panic. (*Yes, readers, you've spotted it! Unbeknown to me, it was Herbert.*)

Deciding that he was (as my mother would say) 'a person under stress' (we get an awful lot of loonies hanging around our library), I decided to ignore him and followed Miss Roberts towards the cookery section.

'I remember this book well,' she said. 'I said to Miss Puddephat when she ordered it in 1963, "Don't bother!" I said. And I was right. No one has ever taken it out since the day it came in. We should have thrown it out years ago, but

19

we've got emotionally attached to it. It's been here longer than most of the staff.'

We reached the cookery section and Miss Roberts took this book off the shelf and handed it to me. I noticed the small man had followed us and now seemed to be working himself up into even more of a panic than before. I wondered if I needed to call an ambulance, and if there was a reward for his return to somewhere.

Anyway, deciding that the sooner I was away from him the better, just in case he was intending to destroy the library single-handed while I was in it, I took the book and went. And that was the start of all my troubles.

2

I was just leaving the library when who should I bump into but my form teacher, Mr Wiggis.

For those of you who are new to all this, Wiggis is a pain in the neck and every other part of the human anatomy you can think of. He came to our school to replace our previous teacher, Perky Parrot, and has been there ever since, like a boil that won't go away. He has been a sworn enemy of mine ever since he first started at our school, just because he thinks that I tried to con him that my Dad would sell him a rare car that he'd set his heart on in exchange for not telling me off for not doing my homework. In fact there may be an element of truth in all this, although I didn't actually say that my Dad had a Morgan car to sell . . . Well, alright, I did. Anyway, the point is that Wiggis has been after me ever since that time to catch me out and get me into trouble. It was bad enough being faced with him all the time at school, but to find him popping up whenever I stepped out on a pavement was too much.

Wiggis glared at me, a thing he always does whenever he sees me.

'So, Boyes!' he sort of snarled. 'What are you doing here?'

'I was getting a book out of the library, sir,' I said.

Wiggis laughed, a nasty sarcastic sort of laugh.

'You?' he said with a sneer. 'A book? Ha!'

I didn't rise to the bait because I have been brought up to be a well-behaved child, even with cretins and idiots like Wiggis.

'Yes, sir,' I said. 'For my mother.'

And I produced this tome on *Gothic Innovations in Egg-White Engineering Structures* and showed it to Wiggis as proof.

Out of the corner of my eye I saw that the small man was now standing just inside the entrance to the library and was still jumping up and down nervously. I wondered whether he went around doing impressions of nervous chickens as part of some Performing Arts Street Theatre and was under contract to perform inside the library. However, my attention was brought back by Wiggis.

Wiggis gave one of his evil grins, which let me know that he had something unpleasant up his sleeve for me.

'I see you have your school bag with you,' he said.

This immediately made me suspicious.

'Er – yes, sir.'

Wiggis's evil grin grew even wider.

'The reason I mention it is because I don't appear to have your Maths homework, so I assume that you still have it with you?'

So that was it! Homework, my most hated and

Wiggis's most favourite subject. But this time I had him. He thought that he was going to get me into trouble for not doing my Maths homework. Well, he was wrong. I had done it (or, at least, I'd copied it from my pal Weed).

'Yes, sir,' I said politely. 'Someone must have put it back in my bag after I'd handed it in to try to get me into trouble, sir. I'd only just found it again, and I was on my way to your home to give it in to you personally.'

Wiggis's evil grin grew even wider. This time he thought he had me.

'In that case,' he said, his smile now so wide in triumph that it was almost splitting his face in two, 'you can hand it in to me now. Can't you?'

And he held out his hand.

'Yes, sir,' I said, and opened my bag. The smile vanished from Wiggis's face as if it had been wiped like a computer screen.

'You mean you've done it?' he said incredulously.

I handed over the two sheets of paper I'd copied from Weed.

'Of course, sir,' I said.

And with that I left him to stare at the Maths homework and secthe silently.

If I had watched and waited I would have seen the small man leave the library and follow Wiggis. Possibly then I would have followed out of curiosity to see what was going on, and then I would have had an explanation as to why Wiggis had a black eye when he arrived at school the next day. However, as I didn't do any of this, I

23

will have to use my imagination again, and use some more dots to show you that this is What Happened Then:

● ● ● ● ● ● ● ● ● ●

Herbert was worried. What had happened to that industrialist, Mr Ruggles? Whatever had happened, the boy had taken the book with the formula and now he was handing a sheet of paper over to the man with the moustache. He must be handing over the formula! Herbert knew he had to get it back, otherwise Bonnie and Clyde would moan at him. He set off after the man.

What struck Herbert as odd, or would have if he had been a Great Thinker, was that the man seemed completely unbothered about checking whether anyone was following him. He was carrying a valuable secret formula just casually stuck inside a cardboard folder along with some other papers. Herbert really felt the man was just asking to be robbed of it. Which was why, when the man decided to take a short cut down a narrow alley, Herbert seized his chance.

The man with the moustache turned into the alley. Herbert rushed in after him, bopped him in the eye, grabbed the cardboard folder and ran off, leaving the man sitting dazed on the ground and wondering what on earth was going on.

Meanwhile, back at the crooks' hideout, Bonnie and Clyde were listening to the irate Ruggles, who was berating them for the fact that when he had finally got to the library, no one had been there to receive the envelope with the money, or

to pass him the slip of paper with the title of the book on it.

'But you were late,' Bonnie pointed out, although she was still wondering what had happened to Herbert. (I bet that idiot went to the wrong library, she said to herself.)

'That wasn't my fault,' said Ruggles. 'As I've already told you, some horrible child tied me up in this phone box—'

Before he could tell them the story again, the door opened and Herbert appeared carrying a folder with some papers in it.

'There you are!' exploded Clyde. 'Where have you been?'

'At the library,' said Herbert.

'No you weren't,' said Ruggles aggressively.

'I was,' said Herbert, 'but this kid came in and took the book.'

Bonnie, Clyde and Ruggles looked at each other, the same thought forming in each of their minds.

'Kid?' they said slowly.

'Yes,' said Herbert. 'He was about this high, wearing a school blazer.'

'It's the same kid who tied me into the phone box!' yelled Ruggles.

'It can't be,' said Bonnie, but without as much conviction as she would have liked, because the same thought had occurred to her.

'A thinnish sort of kid with fairish hair?' Ruggles demanded of Herbert. 'Carrying a red bag?'

'Yes,' said Herbert.

'It is *the same kid!*' said Ruggles.

Bonnie and Clyde exchanged baffled looks.

'What would a kid know about what we're up to?' asked Clyde, bewildered.

'Where did he go?' Bonnie asked Herbert, determined to get to the bottom of all this.

'Some bloke met him outside the library, and he handed over a paper to him.'

'Two of them!' exclaimed Clyde, aghast. 'It's another gang!'

'Not necessarily,' said Bonnie, but again she wasn't entirely convinced.

'Don't forget, the boy knew exactly which book to go to,' Ruggles pointed out.

Herbert nodded in agreement. 'The librarian said no one had even touched that book since 1963.'

Bonnie was worried now. 'You may be right,' she said, anxiously. 'It does sound like a rival gang.'

'And they've got the formula!' howled Ruggles in anguish.

Herbert smiled broadly, proud at having done something right.

'No,' he said. 'I followed the bloke and got it off him.'

Ruggles snatched the folder off Herbert and immediately he, Bonnie and Clyde started sorting through the papers.

'The formula's not here,' said Bonnie.

Ruggles picked up one of the sheets of paper. 'What's all this other stuff?' he asked, trying to make it out.

'It looks like schoolwork,' said Herbert, looking closer. 'Maybe the bloke's a teacher?'

Bonnie shook her head emphatically. 'No,' she said. 'That's what he wants people to think. No, this is a way of disguising information.'

They studied the sheets of paper again.

'$y = 2x + c$,' read Clyde. 'Then $c = 0.4$.' He looked at the others, baffled. 'What's it mean?'

'It's not any formula I recognize,' said Ruggles.

'It's code,' said Bonnie.

'Shall I put the heating on?' asked Herbert, helpfully.

'Not "cold",' snapped Bonnie, irritated. 'Code.'

'We must find that formula!' wailed Ruggles.

'Don't worry,' said Bonnie, thoughtfully. 'We'll get it back. Somewhere here in all these papers is a clue to the whereabouts of that rival gang. All we've got to do is look through them all and find out what that clue is.'

She gave each of them a few sheets of paper, pulled a chair up to the table and sat down.

'Right,' she said, 'Let's start trying to crack the code.'

● ● ● ● ● ● ● ● ● ●

Meanwhile I was having problems of my own at home looking for a tarantula. Have you ever seen a tarantula? It's one of those big hairy spiders and this one belonged to my friend, Bernetta Vincent. Bernetta is possibly the only real friend I've got, mainly because she's such a wonderful dodger herself. She once came up with a brilliant scheme to earn money for a charity: she volunteered her sister for a Sponsored Fast, and then locked her in a cellar for two days and raised an awful lot of money. Brilliant! Alright, not as brilliant as me, but close.

Anyway, she'd bought this tarantula to keep as a pet but her parents had objected and ordered her to get it out of the house, so I was looking after it for her. Or, at least, I was until it got out of the box and escaped. It didn't seem to be anywhere in my room, so I went into the living room and started looking for it there, lifting up cushions and such. Mum was still hard at work on icing her cake, sticking lots of sugary, sticky stuff in the blender.

'What are you looking for?' she asked.

'I've lost a big spider,' I said.

The effect was amazing, she immediately leapt on to a chair as if there was a plague of them crawling all over the house. Honestly, don't grown-ups over-react!

'A what?!' she yelled.

'It's not mine,' I said quickly, not wanting to get into trouble. 'It's Bernetta's. I said I'd look after it for her, but it must have got out of my room.'

'How big is "big"?' she demanded.

I shrugged. 'Sort of tarantula size,' I said.

Mum pointed at the door.

'Get on that phone to Bernetta and get her over here right away,' she ordered. 'I want you both to find her tarantula, and then she can take it home.'

'But her parents don't like it!' I protested.

'*Your* parents don't like it,' said Mum.

I wasn't going to give up that easily.

'It's a harmless pet,' I pointed out. 'David Attenborough has them crawling over him all the time.'

'We are not David Attenborough,' she said. 'Now get on that phone!'

I sighed. There's no point in arguing with Mum when she's in that mood, so I went out into the hallway. I was just picking up the receiver to phone Bernetta, when Dad, who was coming down the stairs, suddenly saw something in the hallway that obviously frightened the life out of him, because he went all stiff. I knew it wasn't me because he doesn't get that frightened when he sees me, only a little jumpy.

'Aaaargh!' he yelled, and pointed a trembling finger at the door.

I looked. There on the doormat was the tarantula. I dropped my jacket over it and scooped it up quickly before it could rush off.

'Thanks, Dad,' I said.

Mum had by now appeared, wondering what Dad was screaming about.

'What's going on?' she demanded.

Dad was still shaking, so I decided to speak for him.

'Dad found Bernetta's tarantula,' I said, showing her my coat.

'Right,' she said, a glint of determination in her eye. 'Get that thing round to Bernetta's now.'

'But—' I started to say.

'Now!' she said.

And with that she opened the front door. It was no use arguing any more. I went.

Bernetta was upset when I arrived with her tarantula, as I guessed she would be. We both knew it would be a waste of breath even asking her parents if she could have it back. Then I had a brainwave. Her neighbour, Mrs Piggott, is a real animal lover and her house is absolutely crawling with cats and dogs and budgies and things. She was the obvious person to ask to look after the tarantula until Bernetta could find a good home for it.

Bernetta found a shoe-box and we punched a few air holes in it, then popped the tarantula in, before knocking on Mrs Piggott's door.

Mrs Piggott opened it with a smile. 'Yes?' she said.

'Hello, Mrs Piggott,' said Bernetta. 'My mother and father have refused to allow me to keep my pet in my house.'

'Oh dear,' she said, very sympathetically. 'That is unkind.'

'I know,' said Bernetta. 'So I was wondering, would you mind looking after it for a day or so, just until I can find a good home for it? It's very small and won't be any trouble.'

'No problem at all, my dear,' said Mrs Piggott. 'I am such a lover of animals, as you know. I will be delighted to.'

And with that she took the box and went indoors. Bernetta and I were just walking away from her door when we heard this scream from inside, so we guessed that she'd opened the box to see what sort of pet it was. Some people are obviously allergic to tarantulas. Then we heard a thud – Mrs Piggott must have fainted.

Bernetta and I looked at each other.

'I hope she didn't fall on the tarantula,' said Bernetta.

We wondered whether or not we ought to go back, but it occurred to us that Mr Piggott might be a bit upset at this incident, so we decided to leave it. As we were walking away we heard the sound of an ambulance approaching, so Mr Piggott had obviously acted quickly.

Anyway, I set off back home, and when I got there I was glad I'd been out. The kitchen was in chaos! I could not believe it! There was icing sugar and everything all over the walls and the ceiling and the floor and all over Dad. It was as if an icing bomb had blown up in our house, and for once it was nothing to do with me.

'Was it terrorists?' I asked.

Mum paused from scraping the icing off the walls.

'I'll give you terrorists,' she said. 'It was this old blender. Dad was just putting all the ingredients in and switching it on when it went wrong and sprayed the whole lot all over the place.'

That accounted for the fact that it was Dad who was covered in the stuff and not Mum. I watched him squelch his way out of the kitchen, on his way to the bathroom.

'In one way it was lucky,' said Mum. 'I needed a new blender if I was going to make proper icing, and I've seen just the one I want in Trent's in the town.'

I hesitated, suspiciously. Why was she telling me all this about a new blender? A new bike, I'd be interested, but a new blender? Then she came out with the reason.

'You can do me a favour,' she said. 'Go down to Trent's and get it for me.'

I was shocked. Have adults no feelings?

'Me?' I protested. 'But I'm all worn out with taking Bernetta's spider back. Also I've got to do my homework. You wouldn't want me to miss doing my homework, would you?'

Mum looked at me grimly.

'How much?' she asked.

I was shocked.

'What?' I said, aghast. 'Sell my homework time for mere money?'

'I'll give you a pound for going,' she said.

Which seemed a fair enough offer.

'Done,' I said.

'Here you are,' she said, giving me four ten-pound notes. 'It's called the DeLuxe Blender. It's in Trent's window and it's forty pounds.'

'Where's my pound for going?' I asked suspiciously. I'd been caught like this before.

'I'll give it to you when you get back,' said Mum.

I was disgusted. 'Huh,' I snorted indignantly. 'There's no trust these days. Fifty pence in advance.'

Mum sighed. 'Alright,' she said.

And she handed over my fifty pence. And with that, I set off.

3

Sure enough, as Mum had said, there in the window of Trent's was the DeLuxe Blender with a big price tag on it saying '£40'. I was just about to go in and buy it when my eye wandered towards the shop next door, Taste Continental Home Appliances. There in their window was the very self-same identical blender (at least, it looked the same) for just £30.99! A whole nine pounds and one penny cheaper!

This was an opportunity not to be missed. After all, Mum had been pretty cheap in just giving me a pound for this errand. Carrying an expensive piece of equipment all the way back home was worth at least ten pounds, and here was my way to raise it, without costing Mum any more money. I hesitated not a second longer. It was my duty to stop shops like Trent's from demanding exorbitant prices for their goods. I went into Taste Continental.

The shop was packed with household goods, all of them much cheaper than anywhere else. On the wall was a huge sign that said 'Mammoth Sale', which made me decide to have a bit of fun with the man behind the counter as he came over to me.

'Yes, son,' he said. 'What can I do for you?'

I pointed to the sign. 'I see you've got a Mammoth Sale on,' I said.

'That's right!' he said jovially.

'Good,' I said. 'I'd like to buy a mammoth.'

His smile switched off and he turned towards the back room and called out, 'Sheila, we've got another one! Throw him out!'

At this a large woman appeared. Hastily I said: 'It was a joke! I really do want to buy something!' I pointed behind the counter at the stock. 'I want one of those blenders.'

He hesitated, still unsure of me, and then said. 'You really do want to buy something?'

'Absolutely,' I said, very aware of the large woman, Sheila, who looked big enough to throw me and Big Daddy out of the shop with one hand.

The manager's face lit up into a big grin. 'Then this is your lucky day!' he beamed. 'You are our ten-thousandth customer, and to mark the occasion we would like to present you with this special gift!'

And with that he reached under the counter and produced the most hideous and most huge pink fluffy toy cat I had ever seen in my entire life, with TASTE CONTINENTAL HOME APPLIANCES printed all over it in big black letters.

'There,' he beamed. 'With our compliments to our ten-thousandth customer!'

I was stunned. Believe me, this fluffy pink cat was the absolute pits. It looked like something out of a horror movie entitled *The Pink Fluffy Cat From Outer Space*.

'I'd rather just have the blender,' I said hopefully.

I was out of luck. I paid up, and then they gave me the blender and the cat and followed me to the door just to make sure I took it with me. I expect they'd been trying to get rid of the thing for months.

Once outside I stood in the shopping precinct wondering what to do. Apart from the fact that the pink cat was horrible, the last thing I wanted was to drag it home with me, advertising to Mum the fact that I'd got her blender at a cheap special offer place.

I decided to dump it in the precinct and leave it, but that didn't work. I'd just put it down on a bench and started to move off when this woman came rushing after me.

'You forgot your cat!' she called.

Curses, I thought.

'Oh, did I?' I said. 'Thank you. Are you sure you wouldn't like it? It goes very well with your hair.'

The look she gave me told me that she didn't think I'd flattered her and she stomped off in a bit of a huff.

Oh well, I thought. And then an idea struck me. I'd sneak it back into the shop. With the name of the shop all over it, no one would think it shouldn't be back there.

I nipped back to the shop, left it just inside the door when the man and Sheila weren't looking, and then set off home.

However, by one of those coincidences that makes life so unpredictable, what I didn't know was the small man who'd followed me around the library was in the shopping precinct with his crooked cronies, Bonnie and Clyde Hipp – and had been watching me the whole time!

● ● ● ● ● ● ● ● ● ● ●

Herbert, Bonnie and Clyde were sitting on a bench, still puzzling over the Maths sheets they'd stolen from Wiggis and trying to crack the code, when Herbert spotted me.

'Look!' he said. 'It's the kid who took the formula!'

'What?!' they gasped. 'Where?'

'There,' said Herbert. 'Carrying that horrible stuffed cat.'

And from that moment my fate was sealed.

'I bet the formula's in that cat,' said Bonnie.

'You're joking!' scoffed Clyde.

'Why else would he be carrying around something that horrible?' demanded Bonnie, at which Clyde started nodding.

'You could be right,' he said.

They must have had a bit of a shock then, because it was at that point that I took the cat back to the shop and dumped it before heading off home with Mum's new blender.

'He's dumped the cat!' said Clyde in alarm. 'What do we do?'

'You tail the cat,' said Bonnie, 'and I'll follow the kid.'

And with that she set off after me, keeping in the background, while Clyde and Herbert

went into the shop to try and get hold of the pink cat.

Unfortunately for them, before they could get their hands on it, it had already been discovered by Sheila. Which, considering how garishly horrible the cat was, is not surprising.

'Here, look at this!' she said. 'That perishing cat's back!'

'That is not a perishing cat, that is a work of art,' said the manager defensively. 'The customer must have forgotten it.'

'Dumped it, more likely,' said Sheila. 'It's horrible.'

The manager was not to be put off. 'It's our duty to the consumer to see that our ten-thousandth customer receives his free gift,' he said. He started looking up his receipts to see what name and address I'd given, and his face grew puzzled. 'Elton John? 10 Downing Street. . . ?'

Sheila snorted. 'No he's not,' she said. 'I know him. His name's Bryan Boyes and he lives in Winterton Drive near my brother. I know because my brother's always complaining about him.'

Of course I only heard all this later as part of the police evidence, but if I had been there I would have complained most bitterly. How dare she spread libellous stories like that about me? Anyway, I found out later that I knew her brother and he's an idiot, and his complaints about me stealing his flowers from his garden and selling them were totally without foundation. I gave those flowers away in exchange for donations to charity (the 'Help Bryan Boyes Fund').

Anyway, back to the scene in Taste Continental.

40

'Right,' said the manager. 'Well you take it up to Winterton Drive, and make sure he gets it. I'm sure he'll be very grateful when he sees it.'

And with that Sheila set off, holding the horrible pink fluffy cat. Meanwhile Clyde and Herbert exchanged glances. Now they knew who I was and where I lived.

● ● ● ● ● ● ● ● ● ●

By this time, so did Bonnie. She had followed me all the way home. Actually if I'd known she was following me I'd have asked her to carry the blender because it was quite heavy.

I took the box with the blender in it into the kitchen, where Mum had finally cleaned everything up and was preparing to have another go at producing her super-duper cake icing. I held on to the box until she gave me my other fifty pence for going, and then passed it over. She opened the box, and then frowned.

'This isn't the same one,' she said.

'It's the new model,' I explained. 'They'd run out of the old ones.'

She examined it more closely.

'It's altogether different,' she said.

'Yes,' I agreed. 'That's because of the new technology.'

Mum looked at me suspiciously. 'If you're pulling a fast one—' she began.

Fortunately for me the door bell went right at that moment.

'I'll go,' I said quickly, and hurried to open the

door, thankful for the interruption. When I opened the door I stopped being thankful.

There on the doorstep was Sheila, holding the horrible pink fluffy cat.

'With the compliments of Taste Continental Home Appliances,' she said. 'You forgot your free gift.'

I blanched. 'Mine?' I stuttered. 'I've never seen it before in my life.'

'Don't you remember?' she said. 'You bought that Special Offer blender for thirty pounds—'

It seemed like a good idea to shut her up before Mum came to the door and found her and the cat.

'Yes, yes,' I said quickly. 'Thank you.'

And with that I shut the door and stuffed the horrible, grotesque, hideous thing behind the coat rack, just as Mum appeared.

'Who was that, Bryan?' she asked.

'Er . . . it was a woman about a cat,' I replied. 'I said we didn't want one.' After all, I am an honest person.

Mum frowned, then shrugged and went back into the kitchen. I heard her plug in her new blender and start to fill it up with all the ingredients for the cake icing. While she was occupied I took the opportunity to open the front door and throw the wretched pink fluffy cat out into next door's front garden. I was just closing the door, when to my amazement I saw this woman (*who I later found out was Bonnie Hipp*) stagger up from behind the garden fence, holding her head where the cat had hit her.

I was baffled. What on earth was going on?

42

Why was this woman hiding in next door's front garden? I didn't have a chance to wonder for much longer, because she suddenly grabbed up the horrible pink fluffy cat and ran off down the street with it. I was baffled. If she'd wanted it that much she'd only had to ask me.

I was just about to shut the door and go back in, when I heard this terrible sound like a blender exploding and spraying cake icing all over Mum and the kitchen.

'Aaaaargh!' I heard Mum yell. And then, 'Bryan!'

I crept back and peered round the corner into the kitchen. My ears had not deceived me. The scene was awful; the whole room was plastered with icing sugar; and the new blender was spread in mangled bits all over the table. Mum began to claw icing off her face, and suddenly she saw me.

'You great big cheating little rat!' she yelled.

It didn't seem like a good idea to hang around to point out that I couldn't be both big *and* little — points of language could be sorted out later. Right now my safety was at stake and I was off like a rocket up our street, with Mum in hot pursuit, covered in cake icing.

4

I won't dwell on what happened next because
the whole experience is too painful for me to
want to remember it. How would you feel if you
were being chased down a street by your mother
while she was covered in cake icing? Really
embarrassing! And when she caught me and
dragged me home, well. . . ! I hardly need to
say what happened next. In short, the usual:
sent to my room, all pocket money withheld until
the twenty-fifth century, etcetera etcetera
etcetera. This last was particularly annoying,
especially with half-term holiday coming up
which is when spending money is most
necessary, as I pointed out to Bernetta the next
day at school when I was telling her how unfair
it all was:

'Honestly!' I said. 'Just because my mum can't
work a blender properly.'

Bernetta made all the right sympathetic noises
about my predicament as a badly used child.
But, as it turned out, she was having trouble
with her parents too. She told me all about it
when I innocently asked her if she was going
anywhere for the half-term holiday.

'No such luck,' Bernetta sighed. 'My parents

say they don't trust me to take me anywhere. It's all because of that tarantula. I didn't know that Mrs Piggott didn't like tarantulas. It wasn't my fault.'

'Exactly,' I said. 'Yet we get the blame every time. Adults are so unfair!'

Bernetta nodded in agreement.

'What did you do with the tarantula in the end?' I asked.

Bernetta looked around carefully, then tapped her school bag.

'I'm carrying it around with me because no one will look after it.'

Carrying it around! She was taking a chance and no mistake. It only needed a teacher to come up and ask to look in her school bag and she was in big trouble.

'Why not keep it in school until you can find somewhere?' I suggested. 'You could keep it in the boiler house. I read somewhere that tarantulas like warm places.'

'That's a brilliant idea!' said Bernetta.

'You'd better make sure the caretaker doesn't find it,' I warned.

'Don't worry,' said Bernetta. 'I'll hide it away safely. And I'll check on it when I feed it. I'll bet you no one finds it.'

Bet! No sooner had she said the word than it set off a chain of thoughts that exploded like a chemical reaction in my brain.

'Bet!' I said.

Bernetta looked at me as if I'd gone mad. 'What?' she said.

'Bet! You've just given me a brilliant idea!'

46

She looked at me, puzzled. 'What? About my tarantula?'

'No, how to get some money. A gambling casino!'

She obviously still wasn't convinced that I hadn't gone mad.

'A gambling casino? How?'

I hastened to explain. 'My Aunt bought me a toy roulette wheel two Christmases ago. I can set it up and invite everyone from school round.'

Bernetta's face lit up. She could immediately see the financial possibilities opening up with this scheme.

'That's a great idea!' she said. 'Can I join in? After all, you'll need someone to spin the wheel. And someone to take the money.'

I thought it over. 'You're right,' I said. 'I'll take the money and you can be the croupier.'

'Or I can take the money and you can be the croupier.'

I decided it was time to point out to Bernetta whose idea this was.

'It's my roulette wheel,' I said.

'Alright,' said Bernetta. 'But where will we have the casino? In the school?'

I shook my head. 'No,' I said. 'Wiggis would be bound to notice. It'll have to be after school somewhere. What about your house?'

'That wouldn't be any good,' said Bernetta sadly. 'My mum and dad never leave. I think they're afraid someone's going to come in and sell all our furniture. What about your house?'

I thought it over.

'My mum's out tomorrow night and Wednesday night at her tap dancing class. If I can get my dad to go out as well . . .' I made a sudden decision. Dad would have to go. 'Leave this to me,' I said. 'I think I can arrange it. After all, this idea is too good to lose!'

That evening I was at home doing my best to recover my Good Image with my parents. I was doing this by sitting quietly reading a comic and watching my Mum practise her tap dancing. Dad was doing one of his crosswords, as always.

(For those of you who are new to me and my family — my Mum is a crackpot who is always trying out new activities. In the past her interests have included bricklaying, motorbike mechanics, hypnotism, karate, steel drum playing . . . in short, you name it, my mum has had a go at it. What happens is, if she reads a book or sees a TV programme about something she immediately wants to try it, which is how the unfortunate cake icing business had come about. Now it was tap dancing. Someone had told her that tap dancing really kept you fit, so now she had dropped cake icing and had gone in for tap dancing lessons.)

Under normal circumstances I would have made a joke about her dancing, like, 'Have you heard the one about the tap dancer? He fell into the sink!' But in view of the recent problems such a gag would have been dicing with death. I therefore restricted myself to a polite and enthusiastic, 'You know, you dance very well.'

Mum stopped dancing and looked at me suspiciously.

'What are you after?' she demanded.

Not for the first time the thought crossed my mind that adults are far too suspicious.

'Nothing,' I defended myself. 'I just thought you danced very well.'

Dad came out from behind his newspaper, keen to get in on the flattery act.

'He's right, dear,' he said; 'you really do.'

This was just what I wanted. I launched into Phase Two of my 'Get Dad Out Of The House' plan.

'It's a pity Dad doesn't dance, otherwise you could do it together, like that couple in those old films on the telly.'

Mum moved towards me menacingly. 'If you're going to say Laurel and Hardy—' she growled.

'No, no,' I said quickly before she could grab me. 'Fred Astaire and Ginger Rogers. I think you'd make a good couple.'

This stopped Mum in her tracks, and I could see that she was thinking it over.

'We might at that,' she said, and she turned to Dad. 'What do you think?'

Dad, meanwhile, had gone back to his crossword and therefore wasn't listening to her, so he just threw in his customary 'Oh yes, very good.'

'You'd like to do it as well?' she asked, pleased.

Dad left his crossword and came back to the planet Earth. 'Er . . . what?' he asked.

'Dance,' said Mum.

Dad nodded, relieved that it was nothing too controversial.

'Er . . . oh, yes, I'd love to be able to dance like that,' he said.

Mum beamed, delighted.

'You should have said so when I joined,' she said.

Dad looked at her blankly, still not sure what was going on.

'Joined what?' he asked.

'My tap class. She takes men as well. And, as Bryan said, we could dance together.'

Dad's mouth dropped open.

'Me? Tap dance. . . ?'

I had him. To knock the final nail in the coffin, I added enthusiastically; 'You'd be absolutely great together. I'd be really proud of you both.'

Mum nodded, all smiles. 'Right, that's settled then,' she said to Dad. 'You can come along with me tomorrow night.'

'But . . . ,' began Dad, opening and closing his mouth like a cod who's been asked a difficult question and doesn't know the answer.

Mum looked at him suspiciously.

'You do want to, don't you?' she asked.

'Of course,' said Dad hastily, 'it's just that . . . that . . .' he stopped, 'I don't want to show you up,' he finished lamely.

Mum dismissed this excuse for the feeble attempt that it was. 'Don't worry, we'll be dancing together,' she said. 'It'll be fun. Come on, I'll show you.'

And she took Dad's hand and pulled him out

of his chair. It was at that moment that the door chimes went.

● ● ● ● ● ● ● ● ● ●

Yes, it's that row of dots again, which tells you that we are going to move back to the three crooks, Bonnie and Clyde Hipp, and Herbert.

Apparently they were still convinced that I had the secret formula, and had been desperately wondering what to do to get it back. Eventually they decided that the only answer was to 'burgle' our house and search for it; the major problem being that we might notice three crooks crawling all over the house while we were having our dinner, or whatever. So the first part of their plan was to call and see if we were in. If we weren't in then they knew they could get on with their burgling without us being there. A very simple plan and one that deserved to work, in my opinion.

● ● ● ● ● ● ● ● ● ●

Bonnie had drawn the short straw and was therefore the one who was now pressing our door bell, just as Mum was about to get Dad tap dancing. At the sound of the door chimes Dad was off to open the door like a rabbit, eager to postpone his moment of tap dancing fame as long as he could.

Dad opened the door and found this woman on the doorstep, holding a clip-board.

'Yes?' said Dad.

'Oh,' said the woman, and she gave Dad a seductive kind of smile. 'Is your mother in?'

Dad looked at her, taken aback. 'My mother?' he said, surprised.

The woman looked a bit closer at him, and then gave a silly little girlish giggle.

'Oh I am sorry,' she said, 'but in this light you looked so . . . young.'

I ask you, what a load of clap-trap! This to a man who looks about 108! And yet Dad, being the idiot he is, fell for it. He gave a modest sort of smile.

'Do I?' he asked.

'You see, we're calling in the area to ask if anyone would like a special new treatment we've developed to make people look . . . younger,' said the woman. Then she gave Dad another of her girlish little smiles. 'But I can see that you have no need of it. I'm sorry to have troubled you. Goodbye.'

Then she smiled again, and left.

Dad came back into the living room, looking sickeningly pleased with himself.

'Who was that?' asked Mum.

'It was a woman selling treatments to make people look younger,' said Dad airily. He smiled smugly. 'She said I didn't need it.'

Mum sniffed. 'I expect she'd left her glasses at home,' she said. 'Now come on, let's get back to this tap dancing.'

● ● ● ● ● ● ● ● ● ●

Meanwhile Bonnie was outside, joining Clyde and Herbert in their car.

'Well?' asked Clyde.

'They were in,' snarled Bonnie. 'We'll have to try again later.'

Herbert frowned, worried. 'I can't be late home tonight,' he objected. 'My mum said I'd got to be home by nine o'clock.'

Clyde and Bonnie sighed.

'Alright,' said Bonnie. 'We'll try again tomorrow during the day.'

5

Next day at school I swung the Gambling Casino into operation. Bernetta and I called a meeting at lunchtime at the back of the school hall and told all the kids about it, promising each of them they'd make a fortune if they only just turned up. (The usual advertising rubbish that all these gambling people use to bring the mugs in.) The reaction was great, with loads of kids promising to bring all their pocket money. That afternoon I started to plan how I would spend the fortune I was obviously going to make that evening.

Meanwhile, back at home, Mum was still practising her tap dancing in preparation for that night's evening class with Dad, when the crooks made their second attempt to find out if the house was free for them to burgle it.

● ● ● ● ● ● ● ● ● ●

The three crooks sat in the car outside our house (as we found out later from the police evidence), while Bonnie put the finishing touches to Clyde's false beard, trying unsuccessfully to make it stick down properly. Clyde wasn't happy with the beard. Apart from the fact that it didn't go with his wig, the moustache kept sticking up his nose.

'I feel an idiot wearing this,' he protested.

'You've got to wear it to avoid being recognized,' said Bonnie. 'And remember, if anyone is in, pretend you're selling something.'

'I know that,' said Clyde. 'What worries me is — say they want to buy it?'

'They won't if you pretend you're selling something that no one wants to buy,' said Bonnie. 'Dancing lessons, for example.'

'Right,' said Clyde, still not convinced, and he got out of the car and headed towards our door.

● ● ● ● ● ● ● ● ● ● ●

As you've guessed, poor old Clyde had chosen the worst possible thing to try and sell, because dancing was exactly what Mum was into at that immediate moment in time, and when she opened the door to him and he announced his presence there by saying: 'Good afternoon. I represent the Edward Tango School of Dancing and we're offering special discount dancing lessons to people in this area,' he was putting himself right on the spot. Instead of Mum throwing him into the road she smiled happily and said, 'Dancing? Oh, good. What sort of dancing do you do?'

This threw Clyde completely.

'Er. . . ,' he said helplessly, while he frantically tried to remember what sorts of dancing there were. 'Lots,' he said hopefully.

Mum frowned, and for the first time she

noticed that the man's beard didn't seem to be fitting him properly. However, just to compare prices, she ploughed on.

'Tap?' she asked.

Clyde, not having the faintest idea of what she was talking about, looked round, puzzled. Tap?

'Pardon?' he asked.

'Tap?' said Mum again.

Clyde shrugged. Oh well, if that was what the woman wanted him to do. Frankly the sooner he was out of here the better. He tapped on the door frame with his knuckles.

'There,' he said, and gave her an ingratiating smile. 'Right, well I'd better be off, but I'll arrange for our Head Office to send you one of our brochures. Thank you.'

And with that he was gone, off down the path as fast as he could move, wondering to himself where this woman fitted in with the Infamous Bryan Boyes, Snatcher of Industrial Secrets.

Mum, meanwhile, was equally worried by this obviously fake caller. Something was up. She said as much to Dad that evening while they were getting their coats on before going to their tap dancing class, and while I was up in my room oiling my roulette wheel all ready for that evening's gambling which would make me a fortune.

'This man pretended he was selling dancing lessons.' she said.

'Perhaps he was,' said Dad, always keen to see the nice side of everybody.

'No he wasn't,' said Mum. '*And* he had a false

beard. I'm worried. Say he was a crook casing the joint.'

'Why would he want to do a thing like that?' asked Dad.

'I don't know,' said Mum. 'It could be anything. Maybe they wanted to check if we were in, and if we weren't they'd try and rob the house. There have been a lot of burglaries around here lately.'

'Yes, I know—' began Dad.

Mum cut him short. 'I don't like the idea of leaving Bryan here on his own.'

'You want me to stay with him?' asked Dad, hopeful of getting out of the lesson.

Mum shook her head. 'No,' she said. 'We'll just have to impress on him that he mustn't open the door to anyone.'

It was at that point that I appeared.

'Impress what on me?' I asked.

'That under no circumstances are you to open this door to anyone,' said Mum.

This puzzled me.

'Why?' I asked.

Mum and Dad exchanged concerned looks, but they obviously Didn't Want To Worry Me (as parents call it when they decide not to tell their children the truth).

'Because you never know who might be calling,' said Dad.

'Absolutely,' agreed Mum.

And with that Mum kissed me goodbye (which was a sure sign that she was worried about something), and off they went.

I waited ten seconds for them to get clear, then I nipped through to the kitchen and opened

58

the back door for Bernetta who was waiting outside.

'Have they gone?' she asked.

I nodded. 'Actually,' I said, 'I think my mum's going even madder than ever.'

'Why?' asked Bernetta.

'She kissed me before she went.'

Bernetta's face crinkled in distaste. 'Urgh!' she said.

'Anyway,' I said, 'let's get the casino set up. The others will be here soon.'

And with that we got to work.

Fifteen minutes later our gambling guests arrived, and thirty minutes later after that the Bryan Boyes's Gambling Casino was starting to show a healthy profit.

Just as I was feeling that good luck was at last starting to turn my way, trouble knocked. Or, to be more precise, it rang the door bell.

'I'll go,' I said to Bernetta who was doing a great job of spinning the wheel. 'It's possibly more punters.'

I went out into the hallway and opened the door, and there on the doorstep were Slug and Juggs, with big, wide, evil grins on their faces. My heart sank.

For those of you who don't know about The Slug (and also Juggs), a word of explanation is necessary. The Slug's real name is Edward Slogg and he is in our class at school. He is about twenty feet tall with fists the size of basketballs and is a bully and a thug. After he had made threats against my life some time earlier, I had put together a brilliant plan which meant that he was arrested for burgling our house and was thrown into a Detention Centre, where they should have kept him locked up for ever, chained to a wall. Unfortunately for me they had released him on some kind of parole, which meant that he was allowed to roam free and glare menacingly at me and make dark threats about getting his own back on me. Fortunately for me the terms of his parole meant that if he even so much as laid a finger on anyone (which included me) he would go back into prison, and this time he'd be stuck in a dark dungeon where rats would be his only companions (which would be very unfair on the rats, in my opinion, because The Slug is a very terrifying person).

The Slug's companion, Juggs, was an idiot who used to hang around with a brainy crooked thug called Wally, until this Wally got suspended from school. As is so often the case in this world, Wally thought I was to blame for his getting suspended and had therefore sworn vengeance against me. Again, fortunately for me, due to his being suspended Wally had to be on his best behaviour, which was why he had asked his thug Juggs to watch me and see what I was up to.

I had been far too lax. Because I was sure that between them The Slug and Juggs couldn't scrape up an IQ of more than 9 I hadn't thought to check that they might have been spying on me. While I was seen to be Good and Law-Abiding, I was safe from The Slug and Juggs and Wally, but if they caught me doing something that might be considered Not Quite Right (like running a Gambling Casino) then I was in deep trouble. As they pushed their way past me and strode into the living room where the roulette game was in full swing, I knew that the deep trouble had arrived.

'Well, well,' said The Slug with a nasty smile. 'What do we have here? An illegal gambling casino, by the look of it.' He smiled at Juggs. 'I think we ought to phone the police. What do you think, Mr Juggins?'

'Absolutely,' said Juggs, who couldn't think without a brain transplant.

The Slug looked down at me, an evil grin on his face. 'Unless, of course,' he said, 'we're looked after. If you know what I mean.'

I knew what they meant, alright.

The roulette session lasted about another twenty minutes or so, and then everyone left, grumbling about how much money they'd lost. We'd done very well; we'd made about ten pounds profit. Or, at least, we would have if The Slug and Juggs hadn't turned up.

Bernetta and I watched as they emptied our winnings into their pockets, smug smiles on their faces.

'Yes,' said The Slug. 'I think that'll do us fine. So, the same time tomorrow night, eh?'

Tomorrow night? If this pair of thugs thought that I was going to the trouble of putting on another gambling casino just so they could cream off all the money from it, they had another think coming! I shook my head.

'We could only do it this once as my parents are out,' I said. 'My parents are in from now on.'

The Slug and Juggs exchanged nasty grins.

'That's strange,' said The Slug, 'because I distinctly heard you say they were out on Tuesday and Wednesday night. So you'd better have one tomorrow night, hadn't you?'

So they'd been eavesdropping on me and Bernetta all the time! Honestly, was there no privacy any more?

'Not if you're going to take all the money, I'm not,' I said angrily.

It was the wrong thing to say. The Slug stopped smiling, grabbed me by my shirt and hauled me about three metres off the ground.

'I'm not asking you, Boyes,' he snarled. 'I'm telling you. You're having another one tomorrow night. And we'll be here. And don't try all that stuff about threatening me with telling my parole officer, because otherwise I'll have to tell the Law about you running this very illegal activity and how me and Juggs were just doing our duty as responsible citizens in trying to stop it. It could even help me get my parole sentence reduced.'

He put me back down on the floor and dusted off his hands, then he turned to Juggs, smiling happily again.

'Ready, Mr Juggins?' he said.

'I think I am, Mr Slogg,' said Juggs.

'Then I suggest we go.' He grinned at me and Bernetta. 'We'll see you at school tomorrow. And here tomorrow evening.'

And with that they left, taking all our money with them. I stood there, glaring after them. All that hard work and nothing to show for it! And, even worse, they wanted more.

'I'm going to fix them,' I promised.

Bernetta looked at me. 'What are you going to do?' she asked.

That was the trouble, I didn't know. What could I do?

'I don't know yet,' I admitted, 'but they're not going to get away with this, you'll see!'

6

By next morning I had come up with a plan to deal with Slug and Juggs. It struck me like a bolt from the blue just as I was waking up. I was so pleased with myself that I could only force down three helpings of Cornflakes before rushing off to school, eager to put it into practice. I didn't have long to wait.

I was leaning against a radiator in the corridor by our classroom, talking to Bernetta, when Slug and Juggs appeared.

'Well, well,' grinned The Slug. 'If it isn't the gambling king.' And he and Juggs laughed, while I did my best to look miserable and vengeful, but unable to do anything about it.

The Slug came nearer and put his huge head close against mine so that he could whisper. 'We'll be round your house just after eight o'clock tonight. Right?'

I sighed, defeated and miserable. 'Alright,' I said hopelessly. 'But come round the back way. I'll leave the back door open.'

The Slug nodded, delighted that this was all so easy.

'Sensible,' he said.

'And there'd better be something there worth

it for us,' threw in Juggs, just to remind us that he existed. 'Otherwise you're in trouble.'

With that the two of them swaggered off along the corridor.

I waited until they were out of sight round a corner, and then I couldn't help it, a huge grin must have appeared on my face, because Bernetta looked at me and said, puzzled, 'What's up? Why are you smiling? They're going to take all your money.'

'No they aren't,' I told her. 'I've got a plan to fix them properly.'

'What is it?'

I looked around to make sure that no one was listening, and then filled her in on my stroke of absolute genius.

'I'm not going to invite anyone over. Even you and I won't be there.'

'What?' said Bernetta.

'Right,' I said. 'I'm going to set the roulette wheel up as soon as my mum and dad have gone out. Then I'm going to phone the police and tell them there's an illegal gambling casino being run at my house. Then I'll nip out. Slug and Juggs will come in the back way, and when the police raid the house they'll arrest Slug and Juggs.'

Bernetta looked at me in admiration.

'That's brilliant!' she said.

I smiled, modestly.

'I know,' I said. 'I'd love to see their faces when the police rush in.'

At that moment the bell went for the end of break.

'I'd better hurry,' said Bernetta. 'I want to feed my tarantula before the next lesson.' And she dashed off towards the boiler room.

'Be quick!' I called after her. 'Remember, it's Maths with Wiggis, and you know what he's like.'

Then I sauntered off towards the Maths lesson, happy and confident in the knowledge that, once my plan had worked, The Slug and Juggs would be safely behind bars and I'd be free of them.

At least, that's what I thought. What I didn't know was that those two cunning low-down rotten swinish cheats had a similar scheme in mind for me. I only found out afterwards because Weed told me – two days later! – that he had overheard The Slug and Juggs talking about that night's gambling casino, and it had gone like this:

'What great revenge!' grinned Juggs.

'Yeh,' gloated The Slug. 'He'll have that house filled with kids gambling, and we phone the police and report it.'

'And then they'll raid it and arrest him for running an illegal gambling casino!' crowed Juggs.

And I was only told this two days later! If Weed had told me about it instantly, it would have saved me a lot of bother. That is the difference between an amateur eavesdropper like that idiot, and a true professional like Bernetta. If Bernetta had overheard such a conversation she would have fed it to me before the words were even dry from their lips.

* * *

However, as you can imagine, I was feeling pretty good while I sat in Wiggis's Maths lesson, despite the fact that Maths is the most boring and useless subject ever invented. I mean, who wants to know why some Ancient Greek who lived ten thousand years ago invented a Law about triangles. I was therefore enjoying myself instead by filling in the corners of all the triangles in my Maths book with little drawings, when Bernetta walked in, late, and looking worried.

Wiggis glared at her, motioned her to her seat, and then turned back to drawing different-shaped triangles on the board. I leaned over so that I could whisper to Bernetta without Wiggis hearing.

'What's the matter?'

She looked at me unhappily.

'I've lost my tarantula,' she said. 'I went into the boiler house just now to feed it and it's gone.'

It was at that moment that Wiggis turned round, saw me whispering and shouted, 'Boyes! Get on with your work!'

Then he turned back to the blackboard again. See how unfeeling and unsympathetic teachers are? There I was, commiserating with a fellow human being and I got a tongue-lashing. Mother Teresa offers help to the unhappy and she gets a medal. It's all so unfair.

It was at that moment that we saw Bernetta's tarantula. I say 'we', actually it was Debbie, a girl who sits at the front, who saw it. She looked up from her book, and came face to face with the tarantula as it crawled up Wiggis's desk and started to walk across it towards him.

'Aaaaaaarrrrgggghhhhhh!!!!!!!' she screamed.

Immediately all work on geometry stopped and everyone looked up and saw the tarantula at the same time. The next second there was a sudden stampede for the door. Wiggis turned round, curious to find out what had caused this sudden panic.

'What's going on?' he asked, baffled. 'Was that the fire bell?'

Then he spotted the tarantula.

'Aaaaaarrrrgggghhhh!!!'

He threw his chalk at the tarantula, which immediately took evasive action and disappeared over the edge of the desk. Now worried that it had disappeared and might be anywhere, Wiggis bent down and started groping around under the desk looking for it, but suddenly realized that what he was doing was crawling under a desk where a huge tarantula was on the loose. He stood up smartly, forgetting that he was under the desk, and banged his head. He rolled clear of the desk, and was then off like a rocket out of the classroom and down the corridor in hot pursuit of our classmates.

Bernetta and I exchanged worried looks. What we had both noticed was where the tarantula was. It was now clinging grimly to the back of Wiggis's jacket.

'We'd better go after him and try and get it back before he harms it,' said Bernetta.

I nodded in agreement and we set off after our mad form teacher. We didn't have far to chase

him. Wiggis had skidded to a halt outside the door of our headmaster, Mr Blake, and had barely paused to knock before he crashed through the door.

'Headmaster!' he panted. 'There is a large spider loose in the school!'

Bernetta and I had arrived at the Head's door by now, and we peered round it. As we expected, the Head gave his usual reaction to stories of terrible happenings in the school: he said, 'Oh dear.' If you told him that the whole of planet Earth was going to be destroyed in the next ten seconds he'd just look worried and vacant and say, 'Oh dear.' We are talking Wimp of the Century as far as our Head is concerned.

'A large spider?' he repeated, to make sure he'd got the story right.

'Yes,' nodded Wiggis, and he held his hands about a metre apart, exaggerating as usual. 'This big. It looked like a tarantula.'

'Oh dear,' said the Head again.

Meanwhile the tarantula in question was working hard to climb up Wiggis's coat and was almost at his shoulder.

'It came into my classroom just now and terrified all the children. I tried to capture it, but it escaped. It could be anywhere.'

'Er . . . yes,' said the Head helplessly, and for a moment I thought he was going to throw in another 'oh dear', Instead he said, 'What should we do?'

'I think there is only one thing to do, Head-master,' said Wiggis. 'This is obviously a dangerous spider. We shall have to evacuate the school.'

At this the Head looked even more worried. If there is one thing he hates more than taking an actual decision it is upsetting people in authority.

'Evacuate the school?' he said, worried. 'Well, I don't know . . .'

Wiggis wasn't going to take any such indecisive nonsense. He took the matter out of the Head's hands.

'I'll go and alert the caretaker,' he said, and he turned to go. It was then that the Head spotted the tarantula on the back of Wiggis's jacket.

'Aaaargh!!' went the head.

Wiggis turned, puzzled.

'What?' he asked.

'It's on your back!' screamed the Head.

The next second both Wiggis and the Head were leaping about the room, trying to shake the tarantula off Wiggis's jacket, and also jumping about in case it should land on the floor. Luckily for the tarantula, when it did fall off it fell by the door and Bernetta was able to grab it up. However, just to keep Wiggis and the Head occupied I threw in a toy hairy spider that I always keep on me in case an emergency trick is required, and they continued jumping up and down as if they were both covered in itching powder.

That night, while Mum and Dad were getting ready to go to their tap dancing class, Mum

72

suddenly asked me, 'What was all this about your school being evacuated today?'

Wow, word certainly spreads fast in our town!

'Oh, it was just a practice,' I said airily.

'A practice what?' asked Dad.

'A fire alarm or something.'

'Mrs Carstairs said something about a dangerous animal being on the loose,' said Mum.

Yes, I thought, Mrs Carstairs would, that nosey old gossip.

'A dangerous animal?' I said in surprise. 'Oh, she must mean Mr Wiggis. No, it was all perfectly normal.'

And I hurried off upstairs to my room before the questioning got more intense, i.e: was it Bernetta's tarantula and how are you involved?

In a way it was a pity I chose that moment to go right upstairs, because if I'd hung around I could have eavesdropped and I would have overheard Mum's next speech to Dad, which would have saved me a lot of trouble. Apparently the recent spate of callers was worrying her. While I'd been at school she'd had yet another caller on some weird and totally unconvincing errand, and she was now sure that a team of burglars was making these visits to check whether the house was occupied. So, as she and Dad were putting on their coats and packing up their tap dancing shoes, she said, 'I don't want to leave Bryan unprotected in the house while we're at tap tonight.'

'Good idea,' said Dad. 'Shall I stay at home and look after him?'

Mum shook her head. 'There's no need,' she

said. 'I've phoned the police and warned them that I think something's going on. I've asked them to watch the house while we're out.'

And with that they put on their coats and left.

As I say, I knew nothing at all about this phone call of Mum's, all I knew was that I was waiting for Mum and Dad to go to their tap dancing lesson so that I could get my Operation Put Slug And Juggs In Jail moving. I heard Mum and Dad call out: 'Goodbye, Bryan! We won't be late!' Then the front door shut.

Right! I rushed downstairs to the telephone and immediately phoned the police.

'Hello? Police?' I said. 'I want to report an illegal gambling den that's operating in Winterton Drive.'

That done I set up the roulette wheel in the living room; then I grabbed my coat and went off to Bernetta's house to make sure I was out of the way completely when Slug and Juggs crept in the back way and were arrested in the police raid. A brilliant plan!

● ● ● ● ● ● ● ● ● ● ●

However, as so often happens with brilliant plans, I had forgotten about Outside Influences. As I'd said before, there were two things that I didn't know;

1. That Slug and Juggs had no intention of turning up, and they had also phoned the police to report an illegal gambling den operating at my house; and:

2.   *My mum, worried about the possibility of burglars, had phoned the police to ask them to keep a watch on our house.*

There was also a third thing that I didn't know, and this was:

3.   *The trio of crooks, Bonnie, Clyde and Herbert, were still watching our house, waiting for us to leave so that they could creep in and search it in the hope of finding their stolen formula. So, when they saw Mum and Dad go off to their tap dancing lesson, and me leave a few minutes later to go to Bernetta's, they were sure that it was quite safe to go in.*

As I've said before, I was only able to piece together what actually happened that evening from the police evidence. Apparently Bonnie, being the most intelligent of the three, chose to sit in the car and keep watch, while Clyde and Herbert went into our house through the open back door to begin their search. They had been in our house barely a minute and had just reached the living room, where Herbert was looking at the roulette wheel, when:

'Freeze! This is a raid!'

And the next second our whole house was full of Police Officers all acting as if they were in one of these American TV police series, coming in through the doors and windows. I expect they would have even come down the chimney if it wasn't for the fact that we had central heating.

● ● ● ● ● ● ● ● ● ● ●

By the time I got back home, just before Mum and Dad returned from their tap dancing, blissfully unaware of what had been going on, it was all over. At least, so I thought. What baffled me, though, was just as I was about to go indoors, this strange woman suddenly appeared in front of me.

'So, Bryan Boyes!' she snarled.

I was baffled. I'd never seen her before in my life, yet she knew who I was. And then I recognized her. It was the woman who'd been hiding in our next door neighbour's garden and had run off with the horrible pink fluffy toy cat. What was certain was that she was very, very angry right at that immediate moment. I wondered whether she blamed me for something, but for the life of me I couldn't think what, unless it was the fact that she didn't like that toy cat. But in that case she shouldn't have run off with it.

'I'm sorry,' I said. 'Do I know you?'

'You will,' she said threateningly. 'You stole our formula, and now because of you they've locked up my Clyde and my Herbert. Well I'm going to get you.'

And with that she was gone.

I stood looking after her, baffled. Her Clyde and her Herbert? Surely they'd locked up Slug and Juggs?

I shook my head and, none the wiser, went indoors, still with a slight feeling of worry. She may well have been just a lunatic, but one thing was for sure, she obviously didn't like me and she intended to do something horrible about it.

7

Anyway, all thoughts of the mad woman from the previous evening vanished the next morning when the post arrived. I was just sitting down eating my way through a pile of toast, when Mum let out a shriek. For a moment I thought Bernetta's tarantula had miraculously appeared in our house, but when Dad and I looked at her she was beaming with delight and holding a letter.

'Listen to this!' she said. 'It's wonderful news! It's about India.'

Dad and I looked at each other. I could see that he was as much in the dark as I was.

'India?' Dad and I said together.

'Yes,' said Mum. 'Do you remember months ago I applied to go out to India to do voluntary work as part of our Third World Group's Campaign?'

'No,' I said.

To be honest I can't keep up with all Mum's activities.

'*I* remember,' said Dad,

'Well, I've got it!'

'Why that's wonderful news!' said Dad, looking all delighted. Then his face fell. 'But . . . that means you'll be going away.'

'Only for a month.'

'A month!' said Dad, looking all heartbroken. 'I'll miss you.'

Miss her? What about the important stuff? I decided to speak up for those of us who had serious questions to put.

'If you go away, who's going to cook my meals?' I asked.

'Your father will, of course,' said Mum.

Dad?! The worst cook in the known Universe!

'Urgh!' I said, just so that there was no mistaking my feelings on this point. 'I'm a neglected child.'

'You're not a neglected child,' snapped back Mum. 'You are a spoiled child. The people I'm going out to help are really neglected. Anyway, there's no need to worry, I'll have a word with Rose Moncrieff. I'm sure she'll be only too pleased to come and look after you.'

Rose Moncrieff? Oh no, that was even worse than having just Dad! Rose Moncrieff is a real flake, a complete out-and-out lunatic friend of Mum's who we had staying with us once after her husband, Edward, left her. I was about to voice my protest, but it was too late, Mum had already disappeared to the bookshelves to start digging out books on India. So I just resigned myself to being a neglected child, stuffed a few more bits of toast in my school bag, and set off for school.

At school I was in for another shock: The Slug and Juggs were there instead of being in jail. I was baffled. What had happened? Why weren't they locked up?

They, in turn, seemed equally surprised to see

me. They started muttering to each other and then wandered off to terrorize some poor innocent kid who was trying to do his homework round the back of the bike sheds.

Anyway, things were quiet for the next few days, mainly because our whole household seemed to be geared to getting Mum ready to go off to India. Despite my protests she seemed determined to inflict Rose Moncrieff on us, and by the Friday when Mum actually flew off for India, it was all confirmed – Rose was coming that next week.

One thing about the Indian postal service, it was obviously better than ours, because we received an airmail letter from Mum on the Tuesday morning. Dad sat at the breakfast table reading it as if it was the most precious thing in the world. Honestly, don't adults in love make you sick! And how anyone could still claim to be in love after being married as long as my mum and dad is beyond me!

'Listen to this,' he said, and proceeded to read the letter aloud to me whether I wanted to hear it or not. ' "It is very hot here in Bombay. It is 115 degrees." How about that! 115 degrees!'

I wasn't impressed. I mean, what did Dad expect in India, freezing snow and ice?

'Of course it's hot,' I pointed out, 'she's in India.' I looked out of our window at the British weather. Damp and cloudy. 'I wouldn't mind a free holiday in India,' I said.

Dad looked offended.

'It is not a free holiday,' he said. 'Your mother is working for a whole month in India to help people who are worse off than we are. I think it's a wonderful thing she's doing.'

'Well I don't think it's so wonderful,' I objected, 'going off like that, leaving me to starve.'

And I just managed to force another two slices of toast into my mouth.

'She has not left you to starve,' said Dad. 'I'm here. And Rose Moncrieff is arriving today to stay and look after you until your Mother gets back.'

Rose Moncrieff! Why didn't adults see that this woman was a hazard in any household?

'I don't want Rose Moncrieff staying!' I objected. 'She's a lunatic!'

'She is not a lunatic,' said Dad defensively. 'She's just a bit . . . unhappy. I spoke to her on the phone yesterday. She's handling her therapy very well.'

This stopped me in my tracks. Her therapy? Don't tell me she was into yoga and was going to be standing around on her head the whole time she was here.

'What therapy?' I asked suspiciously.

Dad shifted uneasily in his seat. Whatever it was, it was obviously worse than I'd imagined.

'Now I don't want you laughing at her while she's here,' he said. 'This therapy has been very useful for her. It's helped her to pull herself together. It's called bucket therapy.'

I looked at Dad blankly.

'Bucket therapy?' I said.

Dad nodded. 'At times of stress she puts her head in a plastic bucket,' he said.

What? Puts her head in a plastic bucket?!

'She is a lunatic!' I said.

'No she is not,' said Dad. 'She says it's been a great help to her.'

I ask you, some adults are so gullible they'll believe anything. If you told them that jumping in a vat of cold custard would make them happy they'd believe it.

'Well I'm certainly not bringing my friends round while she's here,' I said. 'I can just imagine them walking in, and there she'll be, bending over with her head in a plastic bucket.'

'She doesn't bend over.'

'Well what does she do?'

'She sits with it over her head. She says it cuts off the stress situation.'

'Well I think she's completely round the bend, and the sooner Mum comes back from India, the better! The last thing I want is to be saddled with a dangerous loony.'

As soon as I got to school I caught up with Bernetta and told her all about it.

'A plastic bucket?' said Bernetta.

'Exactly,' I said. 'She's raving mad.'

'When's she arriving?'

'This evening,' I groaned. 'I am going home to a mad woman!'

As it turned out, I was going home to *two* mad women, but I didn't realize it at the time.

As I was on my way home from school that evening, minding my own business and still puzzling over how Slug and Juggs had managed to evade the police, a shadow suddenly fell across my path.

82

'There you are, you naughty boy!' snapped a voice. 'Fancy running away from your Mummy like that!'

The next second a hand had grabbed my coat sleeve and was pulling me towards a car. Bewildered, I looked up, straight into the face of the mad woman who'd grabbed me a few evenings ago and threatened me. I was being kidnapped!

I pulled back and tried to break free of her grip, but she had fingers like a steel vice.

'It won't do you any good to struggle,' she hissed. 'Just tell me where it is.'

I looked at her, baffled. 'Tell you where *what* is?' I asked.

'Don't play games with me!' she snapped nastily. 'The formula.'

To say I was baffled was an understatement. I ask you, how often have you had total strangers grab you in the street and demand to know what you've done with a formula? I decided the local mental hospital must have had a clear-out and she was one of the ones to go out on the street, to the danger of people like me.

'What formula?' I asked.

This just made her even angrier.

'Don't pretend!' she stormed. 'I know you've got it hidden somewhere. *And* you had my Clyde and Herbert arrested!'

'I haven't got the faintest idea what you're talking about,' I said. I decided the time had come to call for a bit of assistance, so I started shouting: 'Help! This woman's mad!'

As I say, I started to call for assistance. I had

just got out the first word, 'Help', when she clapped her hand over my mouth, immediately
giving me a problem with breathing.

'I want that formula,' she hissed, 'and I'm going
to get it or you're going to suffer.'

I wanted to point out to her that I was suffering already due to being unable to breathe, but
as her hand was over my mouth I didn't have
much chance to tell her. There seemed only one
way out of this spot. I stamped hard on her foot.
It may be a crude old dodge, but sometimes the
old ones are the best ones, and this was certainly
effective. She immediately let go of my arm and
proceeded to hop up and down, clutching her
foot, while I headed off home as fast as I could,
leaving her to call after me. 'I'll get you!'

Whatever was going on, it occurred to me that
I seemed to be in serious danger from this
woman.

However, on my arrival home this dramatic
encounter receded slightly into the background,
because I got there shortly after Rose Moncrieff
did, and I was curious to see just what sort of
bucket had been prescribed for her therapy. I
mean, did it have handles? Were there holes cut
in it for her ears?

As it turned out it looked to me just like an
ordinary old plastic bucket. She was sitting in
Dad's favourite chair as I walked in, while Dad
was perched on the settee. Beside Rose was this
ordinary-looking plastic bucket, and she was telling Dad about it.

'My therapist said I need to keep it near me

at all times.' And she gave it an affectionate tap.

Like I said, a loony.

'Have you got that because you feel sick?' I asked politely.

Rose glared at me, offended, and Dad moved in quickly to keep the peace.

'Would you like to make Rose a cup of tea, Bryan?' he said.

The obvious answer to that was 'no', but then an idea suddenly struck me concerning Rose's bucket and how I could have a little bit of fun with it.

'I'd love to,' I said with a smile, and off I toddled to the kitchen.

Dad contented himself with making Rose feel at home and wanted. 'I must say, Rose, how grateful both Bryan and I are that you've come to stay,' he said in his most flattering way.

She wasn't impressed.

'If you must know,' she said in a stiff and superior kind of way, 'when Susan wrote to me and asked me if I would, I did find it very inconvenient. My therapist actually said Susan was using emotional blackmail. He said it was very unfair.'

Dad began to look all embarrassed.

'Did he?' he said.

'However,' continued Rose, 'because I am a kind and caring person he said that I should overlook it. He said that I would be a better person for being here. He said that to suffer you was an important part of my therapy.'

Did he, I thought. In that case she was about

to get some really important therapy right now. I returned with a cup of tea for her, and hidden in my other hand a jug full of water, which I managed to pour into her plastic bucket. Unfortunately Rose heard the noise of the water.

'What's that noise?' she said. 'It sounds like rain.'

'It's the plumbing,' I said smoothly. 'It does that now and then.'

Then, with the water in the bucket and Rose drinking her tea, I went and joined Dad on the settee.

'Rose was just talking about suffering,' said Dad, making conversation.

'Was she?' I said, looking interested.

'Yes,' said Rose. 'My therapist says that it is because I have suffered so much that I am the wonderful person I am. He says I have been to Hell and back.'

'Oh?' I said. 'What was the weather like there?'

'I think you have been very brave,' said Dad quickly.

'I have,' said Rose. 'I have been brave and courageous. I have weathered the storms.'

I got up and wandered around behind Rose while she continued to tell Dad what a wonderful person she was. Without either of them noticing, I pulled a paper bag out of my pocket and blew it up. Rose continued with her own self-advertising.

'My therapist says that I am one of the finest people he knows,' she told Dad humbly. 'He says that so long as I have my bucket, I will be an example to the rest of suffering humanity.'

It was then that I burst the paper bag. Immediately Rose stiffened, snatched up her bucket and put it over her head. The water poured down all over her. Dad goggled at her, aghast.

'Bryan. . . ?' he began.

Too late, I was off out of the house before either of them could move.

8

Anyway, that set the tone for Rose's visit, and from then on she didn't have a good word to say about me. She was always complaining to Dad if I even so much as dropped a crumb of bread anywhere, plus she was always sitting down to write reams and reams of airmail letters to Mum saying what a trying child I was and how could she do this to her. Fortunately I made sure that Mum never got any of her complaining letters because I used to offer to take them to the Post Office for her, and then throw them in a rubbish bin instead. All in all I felt that, terrible though having Rose around was, I had things under control. I wouldn't have been so casually confident if I'd known just what fate had in store for me.

For one thing, Wally had returned to school after being suspended. If you remember, he was the partner of that idiot Juggs, and the brains of that pair of thugs. While he had been away, suspended from school, I'd felt fairly safe. Now he was back, which meant that the anti-Bryan-Boyes alliance of The Slug, Juggs and Wally had been reformed, with the brains of the outfit back, and this meant trouble.

As soon as I saw Wally arrive for school I immediately detailed Bernetta to follow him and find out if he had any plans for me. It was lucky that I did, because I soon discovered that, although the good news was that there was a rift in this unholy alliance, the bad news was that all three of them were even more determined than ever to get their revenge on me.

According to Bernetta, Wally had to go to see the Head first before he could start lessons, to receive a lecture on Being Good. These lectures that the Head gives are famous for being the ultimate in well-meaning nonsense. In Wally's case it went like this: 'Now – ah – Walters, although it pleases me to welcome you back, I must warn you that I want no repeat of that kind of behaviour that – er – caused you to be suspended.'

Wally, being intelligent, played the Naughty Boy Who Had Now Seen The Light for all it was worth.

'Yes, sir,' he said. 'That was a moment of madness. I don't know what came over me.'

The Head nodded sympathetically to show that he understood, and that once upon a time he, too, was a rebel.

'I understand,' he said, knowingly. 'The wildness of youth.'

'Yes, sir,' said Wally penitently.

'But it must never happen again,' said the Head, just in case Wally had forgotten that he had Been Wrong (or, that he had Been Caught).

'It won't, sir,' said Wally. 'I am truly sorry. Not just for my actions, but because I let down the good name of the school.' And here he even wiped away a pretend tear, according to Bernetta, which was a brilliant touch, in my opinion. It struck deep to the heart of the Head, who patted Wally sympathetically on the head.

'There, there,' he said comfortingly. '*Humanum est errare*,* as the Latins used to say, eh.'

'Did they, sir?' said Wally. 'Thank you, sir. And rest assured, from now on the honour of the school will be my only thought.'

'Good man, Walters. That's what I like to hear,' said the Head, and with that he walked Wally to the door of his office, adding: 'And remember, Walters. *Absit omen.*'†

'I will, sir,' promised Wally.

And with that Wally left and went in search of The Slug and Juggs, closely followed at a discreet distance by Bernetta, who was keeping tabs on all this. Wally found them just around the corner from the Head's office.

'Well?' asked Juggs. 'How did you get on?'

Wally scowled. 'The old idiot kept talking to me in German,' he said. 'It's all that Boyes's fault. Well, now I'm back I'm going to get him.'

'We've been trying to get him while you've been away,' said Juggs, hoping to make Wally feel good.

'And?' demanded Wally.

Slug and Juggs exchanged awkward glances.

'Well—' began Juggs.

The Slug interrupted quickly. 'He's just been lucky, that's all,' he said.

'Lucky?' sneered Wally. 'What you mean is you

*Latin meaning: We all make mistakes.   †Latin meaning: Steer clear of trouble.

two haven't got the brains to come up with something without me.'

'What?' growled The Slug, and he moved menacingly close to Wally. For a moment Bernetta thought there was actually going to be bloodshed, but Wally had foreseen this.

'Don't come the hard man with me,' he said. 'You're on parole, remember. Touch me and you're back inside.'

The Slug hesitated, and then he said, 'I don't need you to get Bryan Boyes. I'm going to get him my own way. On my own. And you two had better not get in my way.'

And with that he stomped off, making all the buildings around him vibrate. Juggs and Wally watched him go.

'What are we gonna do?' asked Juggs.

'Ignore him,' said Wally dismissively. 'I'm back now. We don't need The Slug. Frankly, he's an encumbrance.'

Juggs frowned. 'I thought an encumbrance was what you have in salad sandwiches,' he said.

'That's cucumber,' said Wally. 'Come on, let's go and work out a way to pay back Master Boyes.'

In other words, I had two different sets of people after me, Slug, and Wally and Juggs, all intent on doing me damage.

Actually, as it turned out I had three sets of people after me, the third set being the trio of crooks, Bonnie and Clyde Hipp, and Herbert. So, in order to catch up with what had been happening to them ever since Clyde and Herbert had been dragged off by the police on suspicion of running an illegal gambling den, it's time for a row of dots again as we enter once again into The Update on Bonnie, Clyde and Herbert's activities (according to later police evidence).

● ● ● ● ● ● ● ● ● ●

Bonnie was returning home, feeling really fed up. All her attempts at searching for the missing formula had failed. And with Clyde and Herbert in jail for the past week, it looked as if their Life of Crime, which had promised so much, was about at an end. It was all the fault of that damned kid!

She pushed open the door of her flat, and then paused. Someone was in there, she could sense it. Perhaps it was that damned kid! Not content with taking the formula for the micro-chip jelly, maybe he had found out where they lived, had broken in and was now after more industrial secrets?

She reached into her handbag and started to pull out a cosh, just in case.

'Bonnie?'

It was Clyde!

'Clyde!' called Bonnie.

She pushed the cosh back in her handbag and rushed to greet him, throwing her arms around him. Behind Bonnie, Herbert had also appeared in the doorway of the kitchen.

'How did you get out of prison?' asked Bonnie. 'Did you escape?'

Clyde smirked smugly. 'There's no prison been made that can hold Clyde Hipp!' he declaimed.

'Gosh!' said Bonnie, looking at him proudly.

Unfortunately the mood was broken by Herbert.

'They let us go,' he said. 'The police lost their notebooks with all the writing in.'

Clyde glared at Herbert, annoyed. 'But if they hadn't let us go, I would have escaped,' he said defiantly. 'To be near you.'

Herbert frowned, puzzled. 'You were near me already,' he said. 'We were in the same cell.'

'Not you, you idiot,' snapped Clyde. 'I'm talking to Bonnie,' And, turning to Bonnie, he asked: 'Did you get the formula back?'

Bonnie shook her head. 'No,' she said. 'I hate to say it, but I think it's gone. The kid must have sold it.'

Herbert was shocked.

'You mean we ain't got the formula after all? And I've just done a week on remand in prison!'

'Exactly,' grated Clyde. 'He may have beaten us on the formula, but he hasn't finished with us yet.'

'What do you mean?' asked Bonnie.

'Revenge,' said Clyde. 'Herbert and I have spent a whole week in the most terrible prison conditions. He has led us a song and dance over this formula. He has humiliated us! We're going to have our own back on him.'

Bonnie and Herbert thought it over.

'You're right,' said Bonnie. 'And we'll have our own back in a way he won't forget.'

● ● ● ● ● ● ● ● ● ● ●

See what I mean? that made three lots of people

after me, all with bad designs on my physical well-being. And, as if that wasn't enough, Wiggis was also working up to blaming me for everything that had ever gone wrong, from the Fall of the Roman Empire onwards. He had had plenty of time to dwell on his experience with the tarantula, and for some odd reason he had decided that *I* was to blame for it. I ask you! How unfair! I only heard about it days after, when Weed told me how he had overheard him talking to the Headmaster, demanding that I be thrown out of the school.

'Do you realize, Headmaster,' he was reported as saying, 'that that fiend in human shape is going to be at this school for another five years. Five years! It'll be like serving a prison sentence!'

'Come, come, Mr Wiggis,' said the Headmaster, trying to placate him. 'I think you're being a bit hard on poor Boyes—'

'I'd like to be hard on him!' snorted Wiggis. 'That alleged child has been a thorn in my side ever since the day I started at this school. I'd like to string him up from the tallest building! I'd like to boil him in oil! I'd like to tear him apart and jump up and down on the pieces!'

The Head was a bit taken aback at this. I don't think he realized just how strongly Wiggis felt about me.

'I tell you Headmaster,' continued Wiggis, 'either that boy goes, or I go. He should be expelled.'

'But he hasn't done anything wrong,' pointed out the Head (and quite right too).

'He has done everything wrong!' stormed Wiggis. 'Look at that tarantula! Look at that business over the Morgan car! I tell you, he is a devil incarnate!'

Strong stuff, eh? The Head, however, would not be moved.

'Even if he is all the things you say, we can't prove anything, and without proof . . .'

Wiggis fumed so much that, according to Weed, he almost expected flames to leap out of his nostrils.

'I'll get you your proof,' he raged. 'I will catch that little swine out. That Boyes has got to go!'

I was totally unaware of all this. All I could hear as I happened to be passing the Head's office was the sound of Wiggis raging. Then the door opened and Wiggis stomped out. He saw me, stopped and glared, and then snapped: 'Take this as a warning, Boyes. I am going to get you.'

And with that he walked off, leaving me baffled. Why was everyone against me all of a sudden? First The Slug, then Wally and Juggs, now Wiggis, and also (unbeknown to me) Bonnie, Clyde and Herbert. I had the feeling that I was in for a rough time in the very near future.

9

The trouble started the next day after school. I had decided to go to school on my bike, so I could outdistance anyone lying in wait to grab me, like the mad woman who'd tried to kidnap me before. I was at the bike sheds after school, unlocking my bike and all ready to ride back home, when The Slug appeared.

'Got your bike here, eh?' he said with a sneer.

And then, before I could stop him, he had pushed me aside, jumped on my bike and ped-alled off. He was pinching my bike! I was furious! I was just about to rush out into the street and call the police and have the SAS go after him and arrest him, when suddenly he gave a scream of fear. I realized that he was trying frantically to control the bike, but the steering and the brakes were not responding at all. As I watched he headed straight towards a brick wall at some speed, and – Smack! – right into it.

I got to the crumpled heap that was The Slug, surrounded by bits of my bike, at about the same time as the Head.

'Oh dear,' said the Head. 'Have you had an accident, Slogg?' he asked, which prompted me to ponder once again on why it is that adults will insist on asking the obvious.

'Someone . . . fixed the brakes and the steering . . . sir,' croaked The Slug, and then he passed out.

'Oh dear,' said the Head, and proceeded to call out, 'Send for an ambulance! Send for an ambulance!'

I picked up the bits of my bike that were recognizable, stuffed them in my school bag, and set off for home, now definitely worried. Okay, The Slug had been injured, but that accident had been intended for me!

That night I mentioned the accident to my Dad. My intentions were two-fold:

1. I wanted to know who had done it, for my own future protection; and

2. I thought it was worth trying to get a new bike out of it.

'Someone fixed the brakes on my bike at school today,' I said.

'Oh?' said Dad.

'Yes,' I said. 'And someone tried to steal the bike but they were seriously injured when it crashed, and it might have been me!'

Dad stopped doing his crossword, the shock was that big.

'Surely not!' he said, horrified.

'They did,' I said. 'I wondered if Rose has been to the school today?'

This suggestion shocked Dad even further.

'Rose wouldn't do a thing like that!'

I had to agree with him that it was unlikely. In my opinion Wally and Juggs were behind it, but Rose was still a possible suspect. Anyone who wears a bucket on her head is capable of anything.

I moved on to the second point.

'I'll need a new bike now,' I said.

Dad did what he always does when pushed into a tight corner, he picked up his newspaper and started pretending to do the crossword again. However, I wasn't going to give up that easily.

'I wonder what sort of bike I should have?' I asked.

'Well,' said Dad, 'a bike is a very expensive thing—'

'I think it's lucky that accident happened to my old bike because it was getting dangerous,' I added. 'If I'd ridden on it much longer I might have been injured.'

Dad tried Escape Ploy Number 2.

'I think it might be best to wait until your mum gets back,' he said.

From India!

'By the time she gets back bikes will have gone out of fashion,' I pointed out.

Anyway, there didn't seem much point in carrying on with it, Dad was obviously set on being stubborn over this issue, so I decided to leave it and attack it again later.

It was next morning that the incident happened that really began to worry me. I was just leaving my house, walking to school, when I noticed a car that had been parked a little way down the road from our house start up and move off as I appeared, going very, very slowly. Crawling, in fact, and crawling suspiciously close to me.

I stopped and looked into the car as it got nearer. Inside it were the mad woman who'd threatened me, plus the small man who'd followed me in the library, and a third man wearing an ill-fitting wig. This was no car with mechanical trouble, these people were after me! To test it I stopped, and then started going along the road in the opposite direction. Immediately the car stopped.

That did it! I broke into a run, and the car started up again. The driver tried frantically to do a three point turn so they could go after me, but they didn't have a chance, our road always has too many cars parked in it. The last thing I saw was the car jammed tight across the road and the three people inside it arguing with one another. I turned down an alley and ran all the way to school. It had been a close shave.

Bernetta was in the corridor when I arrived, and I filled her in on what had happened. I thought it was important that someone knew that I was being chased, just in case I should vanish while I was at school, snatched by these people. Bernetta stared at me, stunned, as I told her about my narrow escape.

'Three of them in the car?' she said.

'That's right,' I nodded. 'That mad woman

who's been after me and two really odd-looking men.'

'But why would they be after you?'

'I don't know! And that's not all. Last night The Slug tried to steal my bike, but someone had fixed my brakes, so he crashed it.'

I saw Bernetta was about to laugh, so I cut in quickly with: 'It's not funny! Say I'd been riding it. Someone is after me.'

Bernetta thought it over.

'You think it was those people in the car that fixed your brakes?' she asked.

'I don't know,' I said. 'Up till this morning I thought it was Juggs and Wally. Then there's Wiggis. He says he's going to get me.'

'Maybe it was him who fixed your brakes?' suggested Bernetta.

I shook my head. 'I don't understand what's going on, but one thing I do know: I'm in danger. There are lunatics all over this place concerned with one thing only – getting me.'

'What are you going to do?' she asked.

'I'm going to fix up an accident for myself,' I said firmly. It had been a decision I'd made on the way to school after my narrow escape. Bernetta looked worried.

'Won't you get hurt?'

I shook my head. 'A pretend accident. It'll be so big that I have to walk around covered in bandages. Then whoever's after me will think I've already been got, and they'll leave me alone.'

'I don't know,' said Bernetta doubtfully. 'Say they're after you for another reason?'

'What other reason?'

'I don't know,' said Bernetta. 'Maybe you've got something they want.'

'I haven't got anything, I'm poor. I haven't even got a bike any more,' I said bitterly. 'No, what I've got to do is come up with a really big accident.'

10

• • • • • • • • • • • •

Meanwhile the three crooks, Bonnie, Clyde and Herbert, were making their plans. At that moment they were in their flat, gathered around a short-list of places where they reckoned I could be got. The word 'home' had already been crossed through, and Clyde was now putting a line through the word 'street'.

'Right,' he said. 'That's those two off.'

'Which leaves just one place,' said Bonnie, and she tapped the third word: 'School.'

'I still think we'll have a problem,' said Clyde. 'If we just walk in there someone's bound to ask us what we're doing.'

'We could always pretend to be teachers,' suggested Herbert.

Bonnie and Clyde looked at Herbert, then shook their heads. Suddenly Bonnie had an idea.

'I know!' she said. 'We go in with a tape measure and say we're from the Borough Council, measuring the building.'

Clyde and Herbert looked at each other, unsure.

'Measuring it for what?' asked Herbert.

'If anyone asks it's for the Architects Department. That means we can go all over the school without any trouble, until we find the kid.'

Clyde's expression of unsureness changed to one of admiration.

'Bonnie, that's brilliant!' he said. 'You're a genius!'

'I know,' said Bonnie with a modest smile. Then her smile turned into one of vengeance. 'And soon we'll be having our own back on that terrible Bryan Boyes!'

● ● ● ● ● ● ● ● ● ● ●

That evening at home, Rose was taking it out on Dad. I think the problem was that I had upset her on one or two occasions over her plastic bucket. Apart from the one I told you about, when I had put a jugful of water in it so that she got splashed (which I thought was quite amusing, and if I'd been her I'd have laughed heartily), there had been a couple of other tricks I'd done with it. One, I'd topped the water gag by sticking a pizza in it and then frightening her, so that when she stuck the bucket on her head she was left with a pizza on top of it. Then she'd got upset because she'd found me with the plastic bucket on my head, walking around doing Dalek impressions ('Exterminate! Exterminate!').

The end result was that after I'd gone to bed I could hear her talking to Dad, and from the tone of her voice I could tell that she wasn't telling him what a wonderful time she was having. Just in case my name came up in the conversation, I crept out on to the landing so that I could listen. In order not to waste time, I took this artificial head with me, that I needed to play a joke on Wiggis the next day. I sat there, making the eyes more bloodshot, while Rose talked.

'I saw my therapist today,' she said, very firm and uptight.

'Oh?' said Dad, which is what he always says when he knows that someone is about to have a go at him over something.

'I told him that every time I look at a bucket now I have a stress attack. He said that Bryan has ruined my bucket therapy. He says that it will be years before I feel I can put my head in a bucket again.'

'Did he?' said Dad. 'Oh dear.'

I ask you, the ingratitude of the woman! Thanks to me she no longer feels the need to stick her head in a plastic bucket, and instead of being grateful she gets all angry about it. And Dad was supporting her! I listened on.

'He has had to come up with a different form of therapy for me which uses no objects at all, in case *your son* does something terrible to them,' Rose continued, now well into her stride. 'He says now, whenever I feel under stress, I'm to start singing. He says it will take away the tension, and your son can't do anything to ruin it.'

Rose, singing? It might take away her stress and tension but it would certainly do ours no good, not to mention our eardrums.

'I'm sure Bryan didn't intend to—' began Dad, doing what he thought was his best to defend me. He didn't have a chance to continue; Rose had a lot to get off her chest and she wasn't going to let him speak until she'd said all she was going to.

'Not that I shall be here much longer to give him the opportunity,' she said. 'I am going. Tomorrow I shall pack my bags and leave.'

I nearly let out a cheer there and then, but it would have given me away. Rose actually going! I couldn't believe my ears when I heard Dad saying, 'But, Rose . . . you can't.'

Oh yes she can, I nearly shouted. I wondered whether I ought to go and pack her bag for her before Dad could persuade her to stay, but I decided to carry on listening to what she had to say.

'I had my doubts when Susan first asked me to look after Bryan, but I never dreamed he would be this bad,' she said.

'I know Bryan can be difficult—' began Dad.

Difficult? Huh, where was the man's loyalty to his son?

'He is horrible,' said Rose. 'The problem is that you and Susan have been too lax with him. You both should have gone to his school before now to see if something can't be done about him. Preferably putting him in prison.'

'We have been to his school—' Dad started to say.

He didn't have a chance.

'His headmaster needs to be told just what he's like,' she said. 'The world needs to be told what he's like.'

'He's just a boy with a sense of fun,' said Dad. 'Honestly, Rose, he doesn't mean any harm.'

It was unfortunate that the artificial head I

was holding chose that moment to drop out of my hand and bounce down the stairs, and then bounced through the open door into the living room, where it lay on the carpet, the bloodshot eyes rolling in it. I heard Dad and Rose both scream, and then this awful wailing began. It was Rose, singing.

Next morning at school, when Bernetta asked me where the artificial head was, I had ruefully to admit that it had been confiscated by Rose and sent to the Director of Public Prosecutions.

'Oh well,' she said. 'We'll just have to get another one.' Then she changed the subject. 'What about all the people who are after you?' she said. 'Have you come up with an idea for an accident yet?'

I looked around to make sure that no one was listening. After all, that was how I had got into trouble before.

'Yes,' I said. 'It came to me in a flash of brilliance last night, what I'm going to do is blow up the school Science Lab and pretend to be in it.'

'*What*?' said Bernetta.

'Ssssh!' I said. 'Brilliant, isn't it?'

'No,' said Bernetta. 'People might get injured.'

'I'm not *really* going to blow it up,' I said. 'I'm going to pretend to.'

Bernetta thought it over.

'But how will you do that without people getting hurt?' she asked.

'Simple,' I said. 'I'm going to set off the fire alarm to make sure everybody gets out of the

building. Then, when everybody's out, I go along to the Science Lab, and get lots of smoke going!'

Bernetta thought it over, still not happy. 'You've got to very careful how you do it,' she pointed out. 'You don't want to actually *get* hurt.'

'I know,' I said, 'and that's where you come in. You always get top marks in Chemistry. Can you think up something that will make lots of smoke and look really good, but won't hurt anybody?'

Bernetta thought it over briefly, then she nodded.

'Yes,' she said. 'When do you want it by?'

I grinned. 'This afternoon,' I said. 'I think it's important that I put my enemies off before they actually really get me.'

What I didn't know was that one of my enemies, namely Wiggis, was watching all this. Although he couldn't hear what Bernetta and I were saying, he could tell that we were up to something.

'I don't know what you're up to, Boyes, but when it happens, I'm going to fix you,' he muttered to himself. 'If the Head wants proof, then he's going to get proof.'

And from his pocket he produced a camera, and took a photograph of me and Bernetta together. Fancy, I was under observation from a spying teacher!

Unaware of this, Bernetta and I sneaked along to the Chemistry Lab at lunchtime and I watched Bernetta put together what she called her Bernetta Special.

'What it does,' she said, 'is make a sound as if it's blown up, but it's not what you'd call a real explosion. However, with all the smoke and things it *looks* like a real explosion.'

'That's brilliant!' I said. 'How did you learn how to do this?'

'I was given a book for Christmas on how to make special effects for films,' she said. 'It's great. So far I've been able to make people think that I've had an arm torn off, and that our house has been blown up. It's really brilliant. I've had to hide the book now because after the neighbours complained my parents want to throw it away.'

She put the box with her Bernetta Special in it behind the teacher's desk.

'There,' she said. 'All you have to do is push this button. That will press these two wires together, and – Bang!'

I looked at it a bit doubtfully.

'Say it goes wrong,' I said, worrying a little for the first time.

'It won't go wrong,' said Bernetta. 'Although I'm not sure how strong I've made it because I've never done this exact one before. Anyway,' and she pointed to a large metal dustbin at the side of the Lab that they kept white coats and laundry in, 'it won't go bang for a few seconds, so you'll have time to hide in there after you've pressed the button, just in case.'

'Right,' I agreed. 'And then I stagger out, the hero of the explosion, with all my clothes blown off.'

'All of them?' giggled Bernetta.

I looked at her coldly.

'Of course not all of them,' I said. 'Just enough to appear badly injured. And that should stop all these people trying to get me.'

That afternoon I put my plan into operation. However, there were two things that I didn't know: one was that Wiggis was still following me around taking photographs, determined to get some hard evidence to prove to everyone that I was a wrongdoer; and the second was that Bonnie, Clyde and Herbert had arrived at the school, complete with a tape measure and clipboards, and that they were now wandering around the school pretending to measure the corridors, while at the same time looking for me.

I decided to carry out Operation Fake Explosion just before lessons started for the afternoon. For one thing it was easier for me to get to a fire alarm to set it off, and for another I didn't want anybody going into the Chemistry Lab and accidentally triggering off the Bernetta Special.

So, at exactly 1.30 p.m. as everyone was on their way to registration, I sneaked away on my own to one of the fire alarm points. I noticed that there were three people carrying clip-boards measuring the corridors, but I didn't give them a second glance, being more concerned with putting my plan into operation. If I had looked at them more closely I would have noticed that they were the same three people who had been after me in the car the previous morning. One person I didn't notice, however, because he was being so sneaky, was Wiggis, who was following my every move, his camera at the ready.

I had a quick look round to make sure that no one was watching too closely (although the three people measuring the corridor seemed to have moved a little closer), and then I broke the glass of the fire alarm and pressed the bell. As I expected, instant chaos! The corridors were suddenly full of children and teachers, all heading for the school yard. I looked round and briefly saw Wiggis being swept away on a tide of children, trying to hang on to what looked like a camera.

I didn't have time to dwell on that right then. My aim was to get to the Chemistry Lab as fast as I could. By the time I got to the science block the school was virtually deserted. All those fire practices we kept having had paid off and everyone except me was now safely lined up outside, being counted. I reached the Chemistry Lab, slipped inside, and went to the box that Bernetta had prepared. I pressed the button as Bernetta had instructed, then made a quick dash for the large metal bin. In case Bernetta was wrong about the timing mechanism and the strength of the 'explosion', I didn't want to be caught halfway towards it when it went off.

I jumped inside the metal bin. No sooner had I done so than the door of the Chemistry Lab opened and the three people with the clip-boards and the tape measure rushed in. Oh no! Hadn't they heard the fire alarm? What were they doing here? And then, with a shock, I recognized them: the mad woman who'd threatened me, the small man from the library, and the man with the badly fitting wig. What on earth were they doing here?

'He's in here somewhere,' said the woman. 'We saw him come in!'

'Right,' grinned the man with the wig. Then he called out 'We've got you now, you little rat! Come on out! You can't escape!'

It was at that moment that the Bernetta Special went off with a bang that shook the whole building.

11

I don't know what Bernetta had put in her Bernetta Special, but all I can say is that I was glad I was inside the metal bin when it went off. Her claim that it would just sound like an explosion and put out some smoke was a bit of an understatement. In fact it blew the door of the Chemistry Lab off its hinges.

As for the three crooks who had been looking so smug and sure they'd caught me a few seconds before – they stumbled blindly out of the lab, coughing, their clothes in shreds, blackened with smoke, and staggered off.

I raised the lid of the bin a little more, and it was then I heard the Head's voice calling, 'Boyes! Bryan Boyes! Where are you?'

Quickly I jumped out of the bin and tore my clothes a little, picked up some of the soot that had been thrown about the Lab by Bernetta's device and smeared it over me, and then staggered out through the Lab door and collapsed in the corridor, just as the Head appeared.

'Boyes!' he shouted as he came running towards me. 'Are you alright?'

I ask you, what a crackpot question to ask! There I am lying on the floor, my clothes all torn

and covered with soot, with smoke billowing out from the Chemistry Lab, and he asks me if I'm alright!

'I'm alright, sir,' I gasped weakly. 'Is the school safe?'

'Yes, you brave boy,' he said. 'We noticed that you weren't out in the yard with the rest of the school so I came to find you. What happened?'

'There were three of them, sir,' I croaked. 'Two men and a woman. I saw them acting suspiciously—'

'I saw them too!' said the Head, suddenly all excited. 'They came past me. Their clothes were all torn and they were covered in soot. I wondered who they were and I went to ask them, but they pushed me aside and ran off. Who were they, Boyes?'

'I don't know, sir,' I said. 'I think they were trying to blow up the school, but luckily I was able to stop them.'

'And injured yourself in the process,' said the Head, and I could have sworn tears appeared in his eyes. 'You brave, brave, brave boy. But don't worry. Lie still. An ambulance is on its way. I'll see that you're taken care of.'

So it was that evening found me, all wrapped up in bandages and the centre of attention at home. (You may wonder why I was wrapped up in bandages when it was pretty obvious that there wasn't a mark on me, apart from smudges of soot. This was because I'd used the old trick of going 'Argh!' and 'Ouch!' all the time I was being examined at the hospital, which meant they arrived at the conclusion that I must be suffering from injuries to my muscles only, caused by the blast.)

Actually I say I was the centre of attention. This wasn't strictly true. In fact, it wasn't true at all, which annoyed me no end. I mean, if you'd done something heroic like save a school from being blown up you'd expect a little bit of attention, wouldn't you? Instead of which I was propped up on the settee like an Egyptian mummy while Rose stuffed sandwiches into my mouth through the hole in the bandages, and Dad and the Head stood around reading the story about the whole thing in the local paper.

'Listen to this. . . !' glowed the Head, and he proceeded to read the bit in the story that mentioned *him*. I ask you, the vanity of some people! 'The Headmaster of Glenwood High School said, "This boy is a hero. If it hadn't been for his brave action the whole school might have been destroyed by these fire-raising criminals. I was personally attacked by these villians as I chased after them."'

'Gosh!' said Dad, impressed. 'Were you really attacked by them?'

Attacked? The old liar! He'd told me all they'd done was push him, yet here he was turning it into the Worst Mugging of the Twentieth Century. The head gave what he thought looked like a smile of modesty.

'Don't worry,' he said. 'Fortunately the old SAS training soon saw them off.'

The SAS! If I hadn't been pretending to be seriously injured I would have laughed out loud.

If the SAS selected people who looked like my Headmaster they wouldn't even be able to defend the country against Noddy and Big-Ears. I was just thinking that surely Dad was too intelligent to be taken in by this rubbish, when I noticed that Rose had stopped feeding me my sandwiches and was now leaning against the Head in a position of admiration.

'I didn't know that you were in the SAS,' she cooed, fluttering her eyelashes.

The Head looked down at her and smiled, flattered by this sudden close attention.

'Well,' he said, 'one prefers to keep quiet about it. One doesn't like to boast.'

Ha! The liar! I thought it was time some attention was brought back to the Real Hero of this incident, namely me.

'What about my sandwiches?' I demanded.

Rose decided to ignore me and instead concentrated on trying to lean even closer against the Head. It occurred to me that if she got much closer to him she'd be on the other side.

'My ex-husband, Edward, was a soldier,' she said. And then she again fluttered the eyelashes. 'Although he wasn't anywhere as near as tall as you.'

'Really?' said the Head – quick, as usual, with the repartee.

'In fact,' continued Rose, laying it on with a trowel, 'you remind me as much of a Guards Officer as you do a commando.'

'Well,' simpered the Head, 'I did think about joining the Guards at one time—'

I decided to call a halt to all this before it made me feel violently ill.

'Hey!' I called, 'there's a hero dying of hunger over here!'

'Here,' said Dad, 'let me feed you.'

And Dad picked up the sandwiches and started to post them through the slit in the bandages into my mouth, while the Head and Rose continued their sickening game of being coy with each other. The Head even gave a little pout.

'They don't mention in the paper the fact that I'm still single,' he said.

Yuck!

However, the next day the Head redeemed himself as far as my heroism was concerned. At least, he did according to Bernetta, who stood outside his window and eavesdropped on a conversation he had with Wiggis. I, of course, was 'too badly injured' to go to school, so instead I had to suffer the pains of my heroism at home, watching TV, and now and then playing a bit of football with a balloon when I was sure that no one was around to see me, because officially I was a complete invalid.

Apparently the conversation the Head had with Wiggis was even more galling to our form teacher because he had gone in to see him with a photograph that he'd taken of me setting off the fire alarm. As far as Wiggis was concerned this was the proof that he needed that I was the villain who was behind every terrible thing that happened in school.

The Head was full of his plans to herald my bravery. He outlined them to Wiggis.

'I have arranged with the Mayor to present Bryan with his bravery medal on Thursday—' he was saying, when Wiggis interrupted, brandishing the said photograph.

'Actually, Headmaster,' said Wiggis, 'I think before we go over the top on his "heroism", you ought to look at this.'

The Head took the photograph and studied it closely.

'It looks like a photograph of Bryan Boyes setting off the fire alarm,' he said at last.

'And that's exactly what it is!' said Wiggis triumphantly. 'I took that photograph on the day of that explosion. He was the boy who set off the fire alarm. This is the proof you asked for that Bryan Boyes is a villain!'

The Head looked at Wiggis, worried.

'Are you sure you feel alright, Mr Wiggis?' he said.

'Of course I feel alright!' snapped Wiggis irritated. 'There's the evidence that you wanted!'

'But this is him setting off the fire alarm.'

'Yes.'

'Saving the school!'

Suddenly the penny dropped with Wiggis.

'No—' he began, desperately.

'Mr Wiggis,' said the Head gently, 'you've had a very trying time lately. Perhaps if you had . . . well, a rest—'

'I don't want a rest!' howled Wiggis.

The Head looked again at the photograph and gave a little smile of pride.

'This boy is a hero and this photograph is proof of it,' he said. 'I shall have it enlarged and framed and put on display outside my office as an example to everyone.'

Poor Wiggis, defeated again, turned and stumbled blindly out of the Head's office and back to our classroom, talking to himself, with Bernetta following close enough to be able to hear what he was grumbling about.

'He didn't spot the fire before he set off the fire alarm because I was following him around and I would have noticed,' muttered Wiggis, still trying to work it out. 'He set off that alarm hours before the explosion, and now he's trussed up like an Egyptian mummy. He is faking it.' And, according to Bernetta, Wiggis stopped and frowned so hard that she thought he was going to bust a brain cell. 'What is that Bryan Boyes up to?'

Later on, Bernetta also came upon The Slug, Wally and Juggs huddled together in a corner and looking equally baffled about what had happened. Apparently their differences had now been patched up, particularly because, as far as they were concerned, I was lying mortally wounded at home. Although, according to Bernetta, Wally wasn't convinced.

'I reckon he's faking it,' said Wally.

'Faking what?' asked Juggs.

'All these bandages and things.'

Slug and Juggs looked at each other, puzzled.

'Why would he want to do a thing like that?' asked The Slug.

'I don't know,' said Wally, frowning even harder. 'That's what gets me. What's Bryan Boyes's game? What's he up to?'

The Slug scowled. 'I'll tell you one thing,' he said menacingly. 'If he *is* faking, he won't be much longer.'

Wally shook his head.

'No, no, you can't do that!' he said.

'Want to bet?' said The Slug. 'I'll spread him all over the school! Look what happened to me with that bike of his. I reckon he done that on purpose!'

Wally and Juggs exchanged brief guilty looks before Wally nodded and said quickly. 'Yes, absolutely. That's what I reckon too. But in this case, if you thump him you'll just make everyone feel more sympathy for him. What we've got to do is catch him out in front of everyone. Prove to everybody that he's lying about being injured. *Then* he'll be in big trouble!'

'But say he isn't faking? Say he really is injured?'

'There's only one way to find out,' said Wally, a nasty smile starting to spread across his face.

'What's that?' asked Slug.

'The Mayor's coming to present this medal to him for bravery at the school, right?'

The other two nodded.

'So, what we do, we wait till he's sitting in his wheelchair all bandaged up in front of everyone, getting his medal from the Mayor, then I release my pet snake. Everyone will get up and start to run, including Bryan Boyes.'

Slug and Juggs looked at Wally in admiration.

'That's brilliant!' they said.

And it was, even I had to admit it when Bernetta told me about it. I always knew that Wally was the really dangerous one because he had a brain, unlike the other two who couldn't rustle up one brain between the two of them. I just thanked my lucky stars that I had Bernetta on my side. Having a brain and two strong-arm thugs may give you the appearance of having the best team, but with my cunning and Bernetta's eavesdropping, we could take them on and beat them hands down! Now I had the information in advance on what they had planned for me, they were going to be in for a surprise at the Mayor's presentation.

However, what, you may be asking yourself, happened to the three crooks, Bonnie and Clyde Hipp and Herbert? Were they badly injured? And did they call it a day and pack up their quest for revenge on Yours Truly?

The answer to both these questions is: no. But to answer them properly I once again need to use my Creative Writing skills (learnt at Junior School), plus this row of dots:

● ● ● ● ● ● ● ● ● ●

Bonnie paced around the living room of the small flat while Clyde and Herbert watched her, worried. They had never seen Bonnie this tense before.

'He obviously knew we were following him, which is why he led us into that trap,' she said. 'But how did he know? And why did he do it?'

Clyde picked up the newspaper again.

'According to this he was badly injured and he's now recovering at home, completely covered in bandages,' he said.

'The poor kid,' said Herbert sympathetically.

Bonnie resisted the temptation to hit Herbert with the nearest blunt instrument.

'He wasn't injured, you idiot. It was us who got injured, remember?'

'Oh yes,' said Herbert. He frowned. 'Then why does it say in the paper that he's all bandaged up?'

'That's what I'm trying to work out,' said Bonnie. 'What is he up to? Why the bandages when we know he's not injured?'

'Maybe he's using it as a way of getting time off school?' suggested Clyde.

Bonnie shook her head. 'No,' she said, 'that's far too simple for this slimy character. We are dealing with a criminal genius here.'

Clyde smiled, flattered. 'Why, thank you—' he began.

'I'm talking about this kid, Bryan Boyes,' said Bonnie. Suddenly her face cleared. 'I've got it!'

Herbert and Clyde sat up as she grabbed hold of them, very excited at her sudden realization.

'Why would someone want to wrap themselves up in that much bandage?' she asked.

'Because they've hurt themselves,' said Herbert. 'When they're not actually hurt.'

Herbert thought this over.

'Er . . . I dunno,' he admitted.

'Exactly!' said Bonnie triumphantly. 'He is using the bandages to hide something!'

'Of course!' exclaimed Clyde, eager to get back to being a Master Criminal in Bonnie's eyes. 'I was just about to say the same thing myself!' -

Herbert was still baffled.

'Why would he hide things inside all those bandages?' he asked, bewildered.

'Because he knows we're on to him and he can't hide anything in his house any more.'

Herbert wasn't convinced.

'I wouldn't have thought you could hide anything worth very much under a bandage,' he pointed out, his brain now working the hardest it had ever worked.

'You could if it was the same sort of thing he stole from us!' said Bonnie. 'Secret formulas!'

'Of course!' said Clyde. 'I bet he's got hundreds of trade secrets hidden under that lot!' He shook his head in admiration. 'You're right, you know. That boy is a criminal master-mind!'

'However, he reckoned without Bonnie and Clyde Hipp and Herbert,' said Bonnie vengefully. 'This is where we get our own back on him. We are going to grab him and get all those hidden secrets off him. We'll show Master Bryan Boyes he can't mess with us and get away with it!'

12

'During all this, what had happened to Rose?'
I can hear some of you asking. Or, what had happened to my mum in India?

Well as far as my mum in India was concerned, not a lot except she seemed to be enjoying herself, although she claimed that she was looking forward to seeing me and Dad again when she came home in a couple of weeks' time. However, the Rose situation had turned out quite interesting. You may remember that she had given up her plastic bucket therapy and replaced it with singing to help her calm her nerves, and also (although I don't know if you noticed it at the time, reader) that she had become quite smitten with our idiotic Headmaster, Mr Blake. Well this attraction to our Head had become quite an obsession, almost as bad as her plastic bucket, especially when she had learnt that he was single. I opened one of the letters she wrote to my mum, and in it, apart from the usual complaints about me, she said that she thought that 'Mr Blake would be quite a catch'. A catch? Frankly if I was a fisherman and caught him I'd throw him back. However, there's no accounting for tastes.

One good thing about Rose's fascination with the Head was that she started to visit our school on various pretexts, which meant that she wasn't around our house complaining about me all the time. Unfortunately, because I was at home, I missed being able to eavesdrop on these visits of hers, but I heard all about them from Bernetta, who made a point of stationing herself outside the Head's office window when she saw Rose turn up. According to Bernetta, Rose's first visit was the best because it led to a major piece of confusion and embarrassment for the Head as far as Wiggis was concerned. What happened was this . . .

The Head was sitting at his desk, trying unsuccessfully to make a paper aeroplane that would fly straight, when there was a knock at his door.

'Come in!' he called, stuffing the badly made paper aeroplane in his desk drawer.

The door opened, and there was Rose, made up as if she'd been involved in a hit and run accident with a Beauty Parlour.

'Hello, Mr Blake,' she said. 'May I come in?'

The Head didn't have a chance to tell her no and throw her out, because the next second she was in.

'I hope you don't mind my calling . . .' she began.

'Not at all,' said the Head, relieved that it wasn't a parent come to complain about the school. 'Is Bryan alright?'

'Oh, Bryan. Yes, he's fine,' she said, giving him one of her best smiles. 'I wondered if there was anything you wanted him to do while he was at home?'

The Head looked at her blankly.

'Do?' he asked.

'Yes,' she said. 'School work that I could take home for him.'

See what I mean about this woman being a menace? Her suggestion certainly puzzled the Head.

'I thought he was completely bandaged from head to foot?' he queried.

'Er, yes, he is,' admitted Rose. Then she added quickly, 'But he could think.'

'Er, yes, that's true,' said the Head, proving that he was as potty as she was. 'I must say, Mrs Moncrieff, this shows great dedication on your part, caring for Bryan this way. Running errands.'

Which gave Rose her cue to turn on the waterworks.

'It is because I have nothing else in my life,' she said mournfully. And here she gave a little tearful sniff. 'I am alone in this world.'

Which, in my opinion, serves her right. Anyone who walks around with a plastic bucket on her head and tries to get me homework when I'm supposed to be seriously ill deserves to be alone. The Head, however, was determined to show that he was a gentleman.

'A lovely lady like yourself?' he said. 'Surely not.'

He had obviously said the right thing, because suddenly Rose started singing, which made the Head go a funny colour and made Bernetta put her hands over her ears outside the window. The Head looked at Rose, bewildered, and she hastened to explain.

'My therapist has told me to sing whenever I feel under stress,' she said. And she looked at him intently. 'I feel under stress now, Mr Blake, but not unhappy stress. My heart is singing.'

The Head looked at her, unsure what to say.

'Is it?' he said. 'Oh dear.'

At this Rose put her hand to her forehead, and whispered: 'I feel strangely faint.'

'Faint?' repeated the Head, worried and frantically trying to remember where the First Aid box was. He didn't have time to do any more remembering because Rose suddenly did a swoon towards him. Luckily for her he caught her just in time. He was standing there, holding her dead weight in his arms and saying 'Mrs Moncrieff . . .', when the door opened and Wiggis entered.

'Excuse me, Headmaster—' he began, and then he stopped at the sight of Rose apparently locked in an embrace in the Head's arms.

'It's not what it appears, Mr Wiggis,' burbled the Head. 'Mrs Moncrieff fainted and I caught her!'

And as if to prove that he wasn't lying he stepped back from Rose, and Rose, not expecting this at all, thudded to the floor.

'I see,' said Wiggis, not convinced. 'I do beg your pardon.'

And with that Wiggis walked out. Frankly, in my opinion the Head was an idiot to expect sympathy from Wiggis, particularly as Wiggis was

still fuming over the business with the photograph of me setting off the fire alarm.

'Wait!' called the Head, and set off after Wiggis.

What happened next I never found out, because the bell went and a teacher shouted at Bernetta to get to her next class, but to me it all sounded pretty interesting stuff.

Anyway, with that out of the way let's get back to the hero of this tale: me, and what was happening as far as my being presented with a medal for bravery went.

Actually I had been thinking over Wally's plan that Bernetta had told me about. (Remember, the one where he let a snake loose in the school just as I was being presented with my medal?) The more I thought about it, the less I liked it. It just showed the sort of despicable person Wally was if he was prepared to treat someone who was injured in that way. I also didn't fancy being stuck there, all bandaged up and helpless, while this snake roamed loose. There was no way of knowing what sort of snake it was going to be – it could be a cobra or a python. I mean, I could be bitten, or even swallowed whole! The evening before I was due to receive my medal, I decided to suggest an alternative to Dad.

'I think we ought to have the presentation here,' I said.

Dad frowned, baffled.

'Why?' he asked.

'I'm ill,' I said. (Although, thanks to the rest I'd been having for the last few days with everyone rushing around looking after me, I hadn't felt so good in years. Though I had to admit, it was a bit boring doing absolutely nothing.) 'Why can't the Mayor come here?'

'Because all your school friends want to see you receive your medal and cheer you,' said Dad. 'And the local press will be there. And don't worry I've fixed up a wheelchair to take you.'

Huh! All this from a man who couldn't organize walking through a door properly. Now he suddenly starts to get organized when my life is at risk from a dangerous snake.

It was at that moment the phone rang.

'This must be more Press people,' said Dad, 'Perhaps even the television?' And he gave a happy sigh. 'What it is to have a hero in the family.'

He went out to answer the telephone, and came back a few minutes later, grinning broadly.

'That was the *Sun!*' he said. 'They're coming along as well. And once the word gets out I imagine the whole of Fleet Street will be there. You're going to be famous! It's going to be a really exciting day tomorrow.'

I groaned inwardly. With Wally's pet snake let loose in the middle of all of it, he didn't know just how exciting it was going to be.

● ● ● ● ● ● ● ● ● ●

Actually, even I didn't know just how exciting it was going to be, because (as I found out later), it hadn't been the Sun *on the telephone, it had been the three crooks, Bonnie and Clyde and Herbert, pretending to be newspaper reporters! Apparently because they were convinced that I had loads and loads of industrial secrets worth a fortune hidden under my bandages, they had decided to kidnap me. Their plan had been to pretend to be reporters, send a car to pick me up as if it was taking me to the newspaper office, and then they'd kidnap me. I ask you, how terrible! It just proves that no one is safe these days!*

Once Dad had told them that I was going to be presented with this medal the next day by the Mayor, they decided that they would change their plan and come to the presentation. They'd kidnap me there instead by asking for a few minutes alone with me for an interview!

● ● ● ● ● ● ● ● ● ● ●

So, with all this about to happen, next day Dad, Rose and I set off for my school and the Mayor's presentation. You may wonder if I felt in any way a bit of a fraud, receiving this medal for bravery for something I hadn't done. The answer is No. In my opinion I had deserved this award many times over for my contribution to the General Welfare Of Humanity. If they were giving it to me wrongly in this case, then it only made up for the times I hadn't been given proper recognition for my good works in the past, plus all the times I'd been told off for doing things when I shouldn't have been told off.

We rolled up at the school just before two o'clock, me still bandaged up and in a wheelchair,

Dad in his best suit, and Rose looking so hideous that I couldn't understand why Dad had let her walk along with us. I had suggested that she walk a bit behind us, like half a mile, but this suggestion had been ignored. What had happened was, because Rose was so intent on captivating our Head with her charms, she had really overdone the Beauty Parlour look. I think even she thought she had gone too far with the six-inch thick make-up, the wig, the false eyelashes, the skin-tight dress, etc, because, just as we were leaving she said, 'You don't think it might be a bit too much? I don't look too . . . forward, do I?'

That was Dad's opportunity to say, 'Yes, you look horrendous!' and insist she stayed indoors. Instead of which he blew it, just because he will insist on being nice to people, and he lied: 'No, no, you look . . . very nice. In fact, you look like a film star.'

This pleased Rose no end. 'Really?' she said, going all coy.

'Yes,' I said. 'Have you seen *Nightmare on Elm Street*?'

However it did no good and here she was with us, trotting along the school corridor in high heeled shoes that would have given any normal person vertigo.

The presentation ceremony itself was going to be in the school hall, and as we trundled along, Dad pushing me in my wheelchair, we bumped into the Head and the Mayor and one or two other local dignitaries who were trying to get in on the act. They were all in a group with the Mayor, as always, worrying about his Public

Image, and they didn't hear us approach at first, despite the fact that the wheels on my wheelchair were squeaking and Rose's high heels sounded like a horse trying to tap dance.

'Now you're sure the Press have been informed?' asked the Mayor.

'Absolutely,' the Head assured him. 'In fact Mr Boyes telephoned me this morning and told me that the *Sun* is coming.'

The Mayor looked baffled.

'His son?' he said. 'I should hope he is. After all, I'm giving him an award.'

'No no,' said the Head. 'The *Sun* newspaper.'

'Oh!' said the Mayor, delighted. 'Really! I wonder how I should stand so that they get my best side?' He looked at the Head. 'What's the name of this boy again?'

'Bryan,' said the Head. 'Bryan Boyes.'

'Boyes?' mused the Mayor. 'I wonder if the family vote for me?'

Not if I have anything to do with it they won't, I thought, and I rolled my wheelchair so that it bumped into the Mayor's ankle. The Mayor jumped and the Head and the dignitaries all turned round.

'Ah, Boyes!' said the Head. 'You're here.'

'Yes,' gushed Rose, eager not to be left out, 'we are!'

'I suggest we go in first so that I can make my speech of introduction,' said the Mayor. 'After all, we don't want the little chap's wheelchair to get in the way of the photographers, do we?'

In other words he didn't fancy being upstaged by a child in a wheelchair. I bet when it came to election time he was only too keen to be seen with ill kids, not to mention dogs and babies and little furry animals.

Anyway, he and the Head and the other idiots who all thought they were something important went off towards the Hall, while Dad, Rose and I went off for a trundle the other way to kill time. I wondered when Wally was going to let his pet snake loose. I was just thinking that I hoped it bit the Mayor, when suddenly I was aware of three people walking down the corridor towards us.

Not more local dignitaries, I groaned. And then I recognized them. It was the three lunatics who'd chased after me into the Chemistry Lab and then got blown up! I didn't need to hang around and ask them what they were doing here; I doubted if they had come to congratulate me on receiving a medal for my bravery.

'I think we ought to go straight into the Hall,' I said.

'But the Mayor suggested we wait for a few minutes for him to introduce you,' said Dad.

'The Mayor isn't about to be kidnapped,' I said.

'What?' said Dad, bewildered. 'Kidnapped?'

And he and Rose looked round to see what on earth I was talking about, just as the three crooks arrived.

'Get the boy!' shouted the woman, and the three crooks flung themselves at me.

That did it. I wasted no further time. Unfortunately, because I was all bandaged up to the extent of having splints on my legs (such was my attention to detail with this 'badly injured'

138

scheme), I couldn't run. Instead I gave the wheels of the wheelchair a shove and hurtled off along the corridor. Dad and Rose, meanwhile, aware that something bad was happening, stood in front of the three crooks.

'What's going on?' demanded Dad. 'What do you think you're doing?'

The one with the wig showed Dad what he thought he was doing by bashing him on the head. Dad sank to the floor. Rose immediately started screaming, and the three crooks set off at a run after me as I raced away along the corridors, picking up speed.

13

While I was hurtling away like I was in a chariot race, Rose's screaming had made the people inside the school hall start to think that something was Not Quite Right. They started to spill out into the corridor, all except the Mayor, who was still trying to make his big speech and impress everyone with what a wonderful person he was. However, once he saw that the newspaper reporters were also hurtling out into the corridor to see what the noise was about, he followed.

Rose was standing there, screaming and pointing in the direction of the three crooks as they chased after me.

'Mr Blake, help!' she screamed, and she threw herself into the Head's arms. 'We've been attacked!'

The Head looked over her hairstyle at the three crooks, and suddenly recognized them.

'Good heavens!' he said. 'It's those people who tried to blow up the school! After them!'

And with that the whole mob poured out of the school hall and belted along the corridor in hot pursuit of the three crooks, who, in their turn, were in hot pursuit of me.

From then on it was like a race, with us all going round and round the corridor system of our school, me in the lead in my wheelchair, the three crooks gaining on me a close second, the Head, Wiggis and the newspaper reporters coming up a good third, and the rest of the rabble just running everywhere like those TV pictures of the London Marathon. We would probably have all been running around in circles like this for days, if Wally hadn't suddenly appeared, clutching his coat close to him and heading for the door. All this was obviously too much for his snake, which he had hidden inside his jacket, and he had decided to head for the great outdoors. He was unlucky. Just as he stepped into the corridor, heading for the door, I zoomed round a corner in my wheelchair and ran him over. He went down with a thump, and his snake was flung from his coat and lay there in the middle of the corridor, slithering and sliding. The effect on the posse behind me was astounding! There was this sound of rapid braking as everyone screeched to a halt at the sight of the snake, their shoes carving deep furrows in the school corridor. Then they all crashed into each other, and all fell over in a big heap.

Me, I didn't wait to see who was going to be out of the pile of bodies first, I hurtled in my wheelchair into an alcove, parked, and watched.

First up were the three crooks, who looked quickly around. They couldn't see me, so they all ran for the door and disappeared out into the street. After that, one by one, people began to pick themselves up and push themselves back

into some sort of shape. Last one up, I was glad to note, was the Mayor, who looked quite a bit flatter as a result of being under the pile of bodies. I watched them cart him off with a feeling of satisfaction, until I remembered that he was supposed to be presenting me with my medal! How dare he disappear like that! Typical of a politician; completely unreliable.

By now Dad had recovered walking consciousness and was staggering around calling out, 'Bryan! Bryan!'

I wheeled myself forward so that he could see me.

'There you are!' he said, and rushed over to put his arms around me. 'Don't worry, son,' he said. 'It's all over now.'

Which, as the three lunatic crooks had disappeared and the Mayor had been flattened, I suppose it was. So the Head presented me with my medal instead, and then we all went home.

After that things settled back to normal. Whatever had happened to the three lunatics who'd tried to kidnap me, they seemed to vanish into thin air. (*Although, as you will see later, I hadn't seen the last of them!*)

I was taken to the hospital for a check-up, where the unfeeling swines reckoned there was nothing wrong with me, so they removed all my bandages and I was returned to school. Luckily for me, Wally was so upset by what had happened to his pet snake (it had been captured by one of the reporters and handed to the police, who then gave it to a zoo) that he decided to stay away from me. This left The Slug and Juggs without a brain to tell them what to do about me, so they went back to walking around the school writing badly-spelt graffiti on the walls and kicking smaller kids. However, I still decided to keep a close eye on them, just in case they tried anything else. (Which, as it turned out later, they did!)

Rose, meanwhile, had a phone call from her ex-husband, Edward, telling her that he didn't want to be her ex-husband any more but her real husband (i.e. he wanted to come back to her). Her phone conversation with Edward was a classic. I happened to be there when the phone rang, so was forced to eavesdrop on it, and it went like this:

'No, I won't listen!' she yelled. 'You are a cheat and a liar! In my opinion you are the lowest person on this earth . . . and I love you. . . .Yes, madly, passionately, heartbreakingly. . . . Of course I will, my dearest darling!'

See? Bizarre, isn't it! And Dad and Mum insist that she isn't a lunatic. Anyway, two days later she was off, back to Edward, leaving me and Dad alone and at peace.

And then, two days later, Mum returned from India.

I've already given you an idea what my Mum is like as far as her interests are concerned. Even something that only lasts a day or two, like cake icing, tap dancing or motorbike mechanics, means that the whole house gets taken over by it, so you can imagine what our house looked like the day after she returned home. The whole place was filled with souvenirs from India. I half expected to find a cow in the kitchen when I came home from school.

Despite all that I was glad to see her back, if only to find out what she'd brought me, and how much it was worth. However, when she announced her gift it rocked me back on my heels in shock, and not from pleasure.

'I decided that I should give you something special,' she said. 'So, I have offered to come to your school and give a talk to your class about my trip to India, illustrated with some slides that I took while I was there. I'm only going to give this talk to your class so that it makes it special for you.'

Mum talking to my class about India, and this was supposed to be special treat for me! Was she mad? I'd never live it down. We'd had other parents before who'd been conned into coming to school and talking to a class, mainly because the teacher was too lazy to prepare a lesson that day. On each occasion it was the most boring thing you can imagine, with people falling asleep at their desks as the parent droned on about stamp collecting or their memories of being a pushbike mechanic in 1927. And the way Mum went on about her hobbies, once she got started with her memories of India we'd be there for days. They'd have to send in food for us!

I decided this called for a plan to make sure that Mum's talk was brought to a speedy conclusion soon after it began so that, mercifully, it would only take a few hours instead of a few days. To this end I hung around while she and Dad put her slides in order all ready for her talk, and then as soon as they were out of the way I switched a few of them around. The results, as I'd hoped, were catastrophic, or wonderful, depending on how you looked at it. As far as the kids in our class were concerned it was great and they all thought it was the best talk any parent had ever done.

What happened was this, Wiggis did a grovelling sort of introduction, telling everyone what a wonderful person Mum was and what good work she'd been doing in India and how lucky we all were to have her here to talk to us. Then he handed over to Mum.

'Thank you, Mr Wiggis,' she said. 'I thought I'd start by showing you some slides I took while I was in India. Now, this first slide is of a herd of water buffalo . . .'

She flicked the remote control to work the slide projector, and up on the screen came a photograph of Dad, Mum and my Gran at the seaside.

The whole class fell about, until they saw the glare on Wiggis's face, which shut them all up immediately. As for Mum, she glared at me.

'A small mistake,' she said. 'I'm not sure what happened there.' However, her look at me suggested she had a suspicion about what had happened. 'This next one is of an Indian Goddess, renowned for her beauty . . .'

She flicked the switch, and this time on the screen came a photo of Dad in his swimming trunks, pretending to be a muscle man. That did it, the whole class fell about in their seats with laughter, some of them even falling on the floor, and not even the look on Wiggis's face could shut them up. I was just grinning myself when one word wiped the smile from my face. It was my mum, bearing down on me, and hissing: 'Bryan!'

I will skate over the scene that followed when I got home. Suffice to say it was yet another case of poor me being sent to bed early without any supper. Luckily I had forseen this and I had therefore laid in a good supply of food that morning, so I was alright.

Next day at school Bernetta asked me what had happened.

'The usual,' I said, 'They acted as if I'd blown up the whole planet and sent me to bed early. Nothing serious.'

'I was worried they might stop you going to Boulogne,' said Bernetta.

I shook my head. 'Not them,' I said. 'They can't wait to get rid of me this weekend, for some reason. They keep checking my health to make sure I'm alright to go.'

'I know,' said Bernetta. 'My parents are the same. You'd think parents would miss their children, wouldn't you?'

I'd better explain about this Boulogne business. A couple of times a year we have a long school trip which lasts a week, and then we have the odd weekend when a school party goes away on what they call a Field Trip. I can never think why it's called this, because in all the time I've been at the school no one going on one has ever seen a field – it's usually to a town

or the seaside. Anyway, this weekend coming it was our turn to go on a French Field Trip to Boulogne, and again, the chances of us seeing a French field were pretty remote from the pictures I'd seen of Boulogne.

This business of school trips is pretty interesting, actually, because I can never really see what the teachers get out of it. They end up being stuck with us for days on end with no escape at all, and yet they still insist on going. I reckon they get bribed by our parents who are always keen to get rid of us (at least, mine and Bernetta's appear to be). Either that or it counts as time worked, like Good Conduct time for people in prison, and they end up being allowed to retire from teaching earlier than anyone else. Anyway, this time Wiggis and the Head were the members of staff going. Wiggis was going because most of the kids who were going were from Class 4P, and the Head was going because no other teacher would go when they heard that I was going.

One thing that puzzled me was that Wally and Juggs had volunteered to go on the trip. This was odd because they were both Fifth Years and yet they were offering to go with us, all Fourth Years. After I had mulled it over for a bit I began to suspect that they had an ulterior motive, and I was right. As it turned out they were going with one aim only, to revenge themselves on me! I discovered this through Bernetta. Because I had a hunch that they were up to something I asked her to use her eavesdropping skills and find out what it was.

(As I have said before, Bernetta is the best spy in the business and even if she only had one ear she could beat the CIA, FBI, KGB, and MI5 combined.) She managed to follow Wally and Juggs when they were in conversation with The Slug in a corner of the school yard one lunchtime.

'Wait till that Bryan Boyes finds out what's in store for him at Boulogne!' sniggered Wally, and he gave an evil laugh.

Juggs and The Slug joined in, laughing along, until Juggs suddenly realized that he hadn't got the faintest idea what he was laughing at.

'What is going to happen to him?' he asked.

'I've told you, we get him,' said Wally.

'Yeh,' nodded The Slug. 'Our final revenge for all the trouble he's caused us. When we get to Boulogne we grab him when no one's looking and we lock him up somewhere safe.'

'Then we come back to England with the school and leave him there!' cackled Wally.

I ask you, what a foul plot! And without Bernetta I wouldn't have known about it and could have found myself in serious trouble. Actually, if I'd known what else was going to happen in Boulogne I might have decided to pull out of the French trip altogether, because, little did I know it, but I was about to come face to face once again with the three lunatic crooks who'd tried to kidnap me before. And this time they would get me!

14

● ● ● ● ● ● ● ● ● ●

*After the three crooks had failed to get hold of
me and all the secret plans they thought I had,
they had given up, left the country and moved to
France, where they had got involved in a racket
smuggling stolen Art Treasures into England.
Frankly it all sounded a bit crackpot to me when
I heard about it, I can't see why people pay
trillions and zillions of pounds just for a blob of
paint on a canvas, and if I knew anyone that
idiotic I'd be round their house with a pot of paint
and a piece of paper first thing in the morning.*

*Anyway, Bonnie, Clyde and Herbert had just
pulled off their first Major Art Theft; they had
stolen a small statue of someone called Sir Hector
Pump from the Musée de la Pump in Toulouse.
All they had to do now was smuggle it through
Customs into England and they would be able
to sell it to a private collector for huge amounts
of money. It all seemed too easy. However, one
thing they didn't know was that they had been
spotted stealing the statue by the Museum attendant. This attendant had telephoned the French
CID (called the Sûreté) describing them and their
car, and Bonnie, Clyde and Herbert were now
under close observation by a French Police*

Inspector called Hercules Oiseau and his assistant, a gendarme called Gaston.

In which case, you ask yourself, why didn't these French coppers swoop on the three crooks while they still had the statue and grab them red-handed? Because, it seemed, this Inspector Oiseau was convinced that Bonnie, Clyde and Herbert were just part of a much larger smuggling gang and he intended to wait until he saw the three crooks actually hand over the stolen statue, when he would pounce and arrest everyone within fifty metres. Apparently he'd got this idea because all the French newspapers had stories saying how English tourists were involved in this Art smuggling racket, carrying rolled-up copies of the Mona Lisa hidden inside their sticks of French bread — proving once again that you should never believe everything you read in the newspapers, especially if you're a French police inspector.

Right at the very moment that Bernetta and I were talking about our weekend school trip to Boulogne, this Inspector Oiseau and Gaston the gendarme were sitting in a hotel room one floor below Bonnie, Clyde and Herbert, listening to the three crooks through a small bug that they had hidden in the crooks' light bulb.

'Qu'est-ce qu'ils disent, Gaston?' asked the Inspector (which is French for 'What are they saying?' Good, eh! Not only do you get Creative Writing in this book, you get French with subtitles as well!)

'Ils someparlentthing de cacher la statue,' said Gaston.

(At which point we shall leave the subtitles and

153

*translate what they said straight into English,
otherwise it'll make this part of the book twice
as long as the rest of it.)*

'The villains!' said the Inspector. 'What are they
saying now?'

*Gaston listened on his headphones, and then
gave a little gasp.*

'They are making their plans!' he said. 'They
plan to put the stolen statue of Sir Hector Pump
into a small red case—'

'Yes, yes!' said the Inspector, excitedly.

'And smuggle it through the Customs into
England . . . through Boulogne!'

*Go on, admit it, you expected that. Of all the
towns in France that they might have used to
smuggle this statue, trust them to choose the very
same one our school party was going to. As I say,
if I'd known that, I think I would have pulled out.
But I didn't, and so I ended up in a lot of trouble.
Although not as much trouble as everyone else,
as you will see shortly.*

*However, enough of this Creative Writing, let
us get back to the Real World, and what was happening at Chez Boyes.*

● ● ● ● ● ● ● ● ● ●

I was upstairs in my room, reading my comic
and at the same time listening to what Dad and
Mum were talking about downstairs in the
living room. I can do this because, unknown to
them, I fixed up a simple system of intercoms
using the central heating pipes. Alright, it's not
brilliant, but it's good enough for me to be able

to hear what is going on when I'm not downstairs. This is a very important thing for a dodger. In fact I would put it at Rule Number One in the Dodger's handbook: always find your opponents' weak point, and this means you need to find out exactly what they are up to. (Your opponents, of course, include everyone else in the whole world who is not you.)

On this particular evening Mum was trying to persuade Dad to lie down on a bed of nails she'd brought back from India to test it. To test it! I ask you! At first I don't think he realized exactly what she wanted him to do, though, because when she said to him: 'Come and help me with this a minute,' he said, 'Where do you want it moved to?'

'I don't want it moved anywhere,' said Mum. 'I want you to lie on it.'

I could just imagine Dad's mouth dropping open in horror as he looked at the bed of nails.

'Lie on it?' he said, his voice quavering. 'But those are *nails* sticking up.'

'I know,' said Mum; 'that's the point.'

'It's a lot of points,' said Dad, worried.

'That's why I brought it back with me from India; to try it out,' continued Mum, ignoring any worries Dad might have had. 'These men lie on these things for days, without any injuries whatsoever.'

There was a pause while I could imagine Dad looking at it, then he said doubtfully, 'It looks a bit dangerous to me.'

'Well it *is* if you do it the wrong way,' agreed Mum. 'It's all to do with yoga. Anyway, if you just lie down on it . . .'

Dad was obviously in no hurry to do any such thing. He tried to keep a conversation going to put off the evil moment.

'What's it supposed to do?' he asked.

'It doesn't do anything, it's to show mind over matter,' said Mum, and she suddenly got all nostalgic as she started thinking about India again. 'That was one of the wonderful things about India. A new way of looking at things, like beds of nails and breathing. We ought to share experiences like that.'

'What, breathing?' asked Dad.

'No, travel. Seeing the world.'

Dad leapt upon this change of topic like a cat after a bird, eager to stop Mum from thinking about the bed of nails.

'Oh, yes. Absolutely,' he said enthusiastically. 'Do you fancy going to Bognor again?'

'Not Bognor,' said Mum. 'Somewhere . . . different.' And her voice got all dreamy. 'Somewhere . . . mysterious. Exotic.'

There was a pause, then Dad suggested: 'Brighton?'

Luckily for him Mum wasn't listening to him properly, which is usually the case with my mum and dad.

'Listen,' she said, 'why don't we go away somewhere this weekend? Bryan's away on his school trip to Boulogne; we have the time to ourselves.'

Huh! How about that! Their poor son is barely out of the house before they're planning to go away. I've often felt that they couldn't wait to get rid of me and this was the proof. This is how they repay me for all my . . . well, for living with them.

'It sounds like a lovely idea,' agreed Dad. 'Where?'

'Somewhere . . . unknown,' said Mum.

I could imagine Dad looking puzzled at this.

'How do we get there if we don't know where it is?' he asked.

'I saw this advertisement in the local paper,' said Mum. 'A Mystery Trip. A weekend into the Unknown with Mystery Tours. I thought it would be just the thing for us. Celebrating being back together after me being away for so long.'

'What about your mother?' asked Dad carefully.

'What about her?' asked Mum.

Personally I could share my dad's doubts. My gran, my mum's mum, is horrendous. She's really old and tough and enough to strike fear and trembling into anybody. I bet when she was a girl she went round frightening dinosaurs and mammoths and things.

'Well,' said Dad cautiously, anxious not to offend Mum, 'she always wants to go with us when we go anywhere. Look at our holiday.'

'Simple,' said Mum. 'We won't tell her we're going.'

'That's brilliant!' said Dad.

'And now,' said Mum, not to be put off any more, 'are you ready to lie on this bed of nails?'

I listened, ears out on stalks, and sure enough, a few seconds later there was this

'Aaaaaaarghhh!!', followed by Mum saying: 'I can't understand it. It worked in India.'

As it turned out, next day my gran came round for tea. I say 'for tea', but in the case of Gran this means about half a ton of food and three gallons of tea. Remembering what Mum and Dad had said about not letting Gran know that they were going away for the weekend on their Mystery Trip, I decided to have a little bit of fun.

We were all sitting in our living room, Dad and I politely munching our bits of cake and watching Gran put it away by the shovelful, while Mum showed her her ten thousand photographs of India.

'And these are some photographs of the Indian railways,' said Mum, lifting up another huge pile of photographs. 'They are something to behold! I took nearly a hundred photographs of the Indian railway alone!'

'A hundred and twenty,' said Dad, though whether he said it proudly or with regret I couldn't work out.

'As many as that?' said Mum with a light laugh. 'It's one of the wonderful things about going abroad, taking photographs. Would you like to see them, Mother?'

'I only came round for tea,' said Gran. 'I'd need a week to look at that lot.'

I thought it was time I made some polite conversation.

'Mum and Dad are going away for the weekend,' I said, chattily.

I said it just as Dad had put some cake into

his mouth. His reaction was instant, he started choking on it. Mum patted him on the back, glaring at me.

'What's up?' asked Gran, looking at Dad writhing in his chair and going purple.

'A piece of cake just went down the wrong way,' said Mum.

Dad nodded, recovering. I decided not to let them off the hook that easily, I waited to see how they were going to get out of having Gran go with them on their weekend Mystery Trip. It would pay them back for sending me to bed early without any supper.

'You *are* going away at the weekend, aren't you?' I asked innocently.

Mum and Dad both glared at me.

'Have you tidied up your room?' snapped Mum.

'Actually,' said Gran, '*I'm* going away this weekend, too.'

Oh, pity, I thought, and I grabbed a piece of cake.

'You are?' said Dad politely, interested now that he and Mum were safe from having Gran with them. 'Where to?'

'The French coast,' said Gran.

This time it was my turn to choke. The French coast! It would be just my luck if she was going to Boulogne and I had to spend the weekend avoiding her.

Dad patted me on the back as I coughed the bit of cake up. Gran looked at the rest of the cake on the plate suspiciously.

'What's wrong with this cake?' she demanded.

'Nothing,' said Mum defensively.

'Then why is everyone choking on it?' Gran demanded.

'You aren't going to Boulogne?' I asked hopefully.

Gran shook her head. 'No,' she said. 'Calais,' and I could breathe again.

Then Gran made the point that she'd been wanting to make all evening.

'My friend Ethel fixed it up,' she said, adding pointedly, 'She says she knows my own family don't want me with them, so we're going on a weekend trip to Calais. We leave tomorrow evening.'

Eager to get rid of these accusations of guilt, Mum said: 'Bryan's going to Boulogne with his school tomorrow evening for the weekend.'

Gran wasn't to be put off.

'And where are you two going without me?' she asked.

'It's a Mystery Trip,' said Dad.

'We were going to ask you if you'd like to come with us,' said Mum, now safe in the knowledge that Gran wasn't free to come.

'Oh, yes,' agreed Dad, 'but now you're going to Calais . . .'

And he took another piece of cake and started munching it happily, while Mum started to show Gran the photographs of the Indian railways. I ask you, what a pair of hypocrites!

I told Bernetta about them the next day while we were waiting to start our extra French lesson in preparation for the French trip.

'And then they said they were going to invite

161

her to go with them!' I said, outraged. 'What a couple of hypocrites!'

'I know,' agreed Bernetta. 'Adults are terrible liars. I tell my parents that they're a bad example to me.'

'What do they say to that?' I asked.

'They tell me to go to my room,' said Bernetta.

'Same here,' I sympathized. 'If parents had their way we'd all be locked in our rooms, like in one of those horror films.'

Just then Wiggis arrived and we all pretended to look interested.

'Now, as you all know, tomorrow we are all going to Boulogne for the weekend,' said Wiggis, stating the obvious as teachers love to do. 'I therefore thought it a good idea to brush up our French. Or, as they say in France, *rafraîchir notre Français.*'

He looked at us to see if we were impressed by this display of terrible French, then he continued. 'We will start with some phrases for use in ordinary situations. Imagine you are on a bus.'

Immediately we all started making bus noises in French, sort of 'Vrrroom vroom!'

'Quiet!' yelled Wiggis, and the buses stopped. 'Now, I am a passenger and you are all bus conductors.'

'Does one French bus really have all this many bus conductors on it, sir?' I asked innocently.

'Shut up, Boyes, or there will be one conductor less,' snapped Wiggis. 'Now, Slogg. *Cet autobus va-t-il à la gare?*'

Everyone in the class turned to look at The Slug, who stared blankly back at Wiggis.

'What?' asked The Slug, not having the faintest idea what Wiggis was talking about.

' "Does this bus go to the station?" ' translated Wiggis.

The Slug frowned. 'What number bus is it?' he asked.

This time it was Wiggis's turn to look baffled.

'What do you mean, "What number bus is it?" ' he asked.

'Well if it's a 39 it does,' said The Slug.

Wiggis glared at him, annoyed.

'This isn't a 39,' he said in irritation.

At which all the rest of us said in chorus: '*Non. Cet autobus* doesn't go to the station.'

'Shut up!' shouted Wiggis, beginning to lose his temper. 'We are talking about a hypothetical bus!'

'Where does a hypothetical bus go?' I asked.

'It doesn't go anywhere!' said Wiggis, at which we all again chanted in chorus: '*Non. Cet autobus* doesn't go to the station.'

'Quiet!' shouted Wiggis. 'We will start again.' This time he turned to Bernetta. 'Vincent. *Allez-vous à la gare?*'

Bernetta looked back at him, baffled. 'Pardon, sir?' she asked.

' "Are you going to the station?" ' Wiggis translated.

Bernetta thought it over. 'Er . . . *oui*,' she decided.

'*Bon*,' said Wiggis, pleased.

'*Par taxi*,' I added.

Wiggis came over to my desk and scowled at me.

'And why, Boyes,' he demanded, 'would Vincent want to go to *la gare* by taxi?'

'Because the bus doesn't go anywhere, sir,' I pointed out. 'Remember, you said so.'

'A 38 goes near the station,' suggested The Slug, helpfully, completely out of his depth.

'I don't want to know about the 38 bus!' stormed Wiggis. He stood, recovering his temper for a few seconds, and then said: 'Right, let's get on.'

'Get on what, sir?' I asked.

'This rotten bus!' Wiggis raged, building up to boiling point again.

I shook my head. 'I don't think that's a good idea, sir,' I said.

'And why don't you think it is a good idea?' demanded Wiggis, and once again the whole class chanted: 'Because this bus does not go to the station.'

'Aaaaargghhhh!!' shouted Wiggis, and with that he stormed out of the classroom.

It just goes to show that some adults have no sense of humour.

Anyway, that evening, with all of our school party now totally fluent in the French language after this one lesson, we climbed aboard our coach to set off for Folkestone and the ferry to Boulogne. As the coach started up we looked out of the window at our parents as they waved us their tearful goodbyes (although it looked to me as if an awful lot of them were smiling a bit widely at the thought of getting rid of their offspring for two whole days). The only adult who seemed to look really gloomy was

Wiggis. The Head, being an idiot, looked as if he was going to enjoy the whole thing.

'Boulogne, here we come!' he called happily, and the engine of the coach revved up, and we were off.

15

The trip to Boulogne was pretty uneventful, really. No one got sick on the coach to Folkestone, and only six people were sick on the ferry crossing the Channel, and that was because they'd eaten too much. The real shocks came when we actually got to Boulogne. We were standing around in the Arrivals place, doing our best to annoy the Customs officials by calling out, 'Are you sure the gold bars are safe inside your bag, Mr Wiggis?' and things like that, when who should I see but my Gran with her friend Ethel! I couldn't believe it! She was supposed to be in Calais!

I hid behind the Head as Gran and Ethel went past, running people over with their luggage trolley. Gran was muttering: 'Well I think it's a bit much! If I'd wanted to go to Boulogne I'd have booked to go to Boulogne. I wanted to go to Calais. I've a good mind to sue the coach firm.'

'It's not their fault there's an industrial dispute at Calais,' pointed out Ethel. 'And Boulogne is still France.'

'Yes, but my horrible grandson's here for the weekend with his rotten school,' said Gran, and they disappeared to go and harass some poor French Customs Officer.

I was outraged. Horrible grandson? What a way to describe someone who's been as good to her as I have. I was just about to step out from behind the cover of the Head, when who should appear off another ferry but my mum and dad! They looked absolutely stunned, Mum especially.

'I still can't get over it!' she said. 'Boulogne of all places!'

'Well it is a Mystery Trip,' said Dad.

Mum shook her head as if in a daze and they walked on towards the Customs. By this time Wiggis and the Head had sorted out what we were supposed to be doing and we all moved forward.

'Did you see that?' I said to Bernetta.

'What?' she asked.

'My mum and dad and my gran are here as well,' I groaned. 'Everybody's in Boulogne this weekend!'

● ● ● ● ● ● ● ● ●

I didn't know just how right I was, because unknown to me, also in the Arrivals lounge at the same time as all of us were the three crooks, Bonnie, Clyde and Herbert, 'casing the joint' for their devious dealings. I didn't see them because they had already spotted me and were now hiding behind a column, pointing at me. I only found out about this afterwards from the evidence of the French Police (namely Inspector Oiseau and Gaston the gendarme, who were also in the Arrivals lounge, keeping watch on the three crooks).

'Did you notice all that, Gaston?' said the Inspector to his assistant.

'All what, m'sieur l'Inspecteur?' asked Gaston.

'That business with the English tourists. I noticed with my trained eye that the three English crooks recognize that man and that woman who came through just now.'

'Oui,' agreed Gaston.

'And also that they are now pointing to that party of school children. Therefore, I deduce that their smuggling contact is either that man and that woman, or one of that school party.'

'The school party?' said Gaston, shocked. 'But they are only children!'

'Children and teachers,' pointed out the Inspector. 'Note how suspicious the two men with them look, particularly the one with the moustache [Wiggis]. Mark my words, Gaston, if we follow them and keep a close eye on that lot, then not only shall we recover the stolen statue of Sir Hector Pump and be the heroes of all France, we shall also catch the whole smuggling gang in one go!'

'Magnifique!' said Gaston, impressed. 'What do we do now?'

'We follow them and find out which hotels they are all staying in, and then we watch. And, when we have watched and they make their move, we pounce!'

● ● ● ● ● ● ● ● ● ●

As it turned out, the Inspector's job of watching was made a lot easier than it could have been, because, as coincidence would have it, we all booked into the same little hotel. Yes, all of us; Dad and Mum, Gran and Ethel, and our school party. This was mainly because it was the only one that had any rooms vacant. It also turned out to be the very self-same hotel where Bonnie, Clyde and Herbert were staying. By the time the Inspector and Gaston had also booked in, under cover, the hotel was full, and from that moment on chaos descended upon this poor French seaside town.

The cause of the chaos was four little red suitcases. If you remember (though I doubt if you do, which is why I'm reminding you), the three crooks had the stolen statue of Sir Hector Pump hidden inside a small red suitcase. Well, at the same time in that hotel there were another three identical red suitcases floating around, as follows:

Gran had an identical red suitcase with all her emergency supplies of food in.

Mum had an identical red suitcase with all her overnight things in (nightdress, etc). This was not such a coincidence, because it had been a Christmas present from Gran. Gran had bought two for the price of one at a sale, and had kept one herself and given the other to Mum.

Wiggis had an identical red suitcase which contained all the work sheets for this Boulogne trip.

So, have you got that? Four identical red suitcases: the crooks' one containing the stolen statue of Sir Hector Pump; Gran's containing food; Mum's containing her nightdress and stuff; and Wiggis's containing school work sheets. It is important to remember all this because someone will be asking questions afterwards, and that person will be Inspector Hercules Oiseau of the French Sûreté, who is trying to recover the stolen statue.

• • • • • • • • • •

As far as the three crooks were concerned, their main aim was to stash the stolen statue away somewhere safe so that I couldn't get at it. Within a few moments of getting back to the hotel they were in their rooms and Bonnie was stuffing the statue tightly inside her little red case.

'Maybe it's a coincidence that the kid and his school party have booked in here?' suggested Clyde.

'And his parents as well?' said Bonnie. 'Don't you believe it! We both know that kid is no ordinary kid, he is a criminal mastermind. Look what happened to us when we ran into him in England.'

'True,' admitted Clyde, ruefully.

'Somehow he's found out where we're staying and what we're up to,' said Bonnie, closing the little red case. 'That can only mean one thing. He is going to take this statue from us the same way he stole that formula.'

She held out the case to Herbert.

'Herbert,' she said, 'take this down to the Hotel Reception and get them to put it in the safe. That

172

Bryan Boyes fiend will never think of looking for it there!'

● ● ● ● ● ● ● ● ● ●

Meanwhile, of more interest to me was what Wally, Slug and Juggs were up to. If you recall they had plans to get rid of me when we all got to Boulogne. As Bernetta and I listened outside their hotel room, we heard Wally outline them.

'I've checked this place out,' said Wally. 'There's a toilet on the top floor. We go now and grab hold of Bryan Boyes and then we lock him in that.'

'That won't hold him,' The Slug objected. 'He'll be out of there as soon as someone else wants to use it.'

Wally gave a sly grin. 'No he won't,' he said. 'I've already stuck a sign on it saying "Out of order". By the time anyone realizes it isn't really out of order, the weekend'll be over and we'll be back in England, *without* Master Bryan Boyes.'

The idea filtered through to Slug's and Juggs's brains, and they started to smile too.

'That's brilliant!' said The Slug.

Bernetta and I decided it was time for us to sneak off, just in case they put their plan into operation straight away and found us outside their room.

'What are you going to do?' asked Bernetta.

'Simple,' I said. 'They want to get me, then we let them get me.'

'What?' said Bernetta, astonished.

'I've got a plan,' I said. And I told it to her.

So it was that when Wally, Slug and Juggs came looking for me a few minutes later they found Bernetta standing beside an open door.

'You seen Bryan Boyes?' they asked her.

'Yes,' said Bernetta. 'I'm waiting for him. He's in there, in the toilet.' And she indicated the open door.

Wally, Slug and Juggs exchanged mean looks.

'Well you can stop waiting for him,' said Wally. 'We want to have a quiet word with him.'

'But—' began Bernetta.

'No *buts*. Buzz off,' said Slug nastily.

Bernetta hesitated, then she went. Wally, Slug and Juggs grinned at each other, and walked into the toilet. As soon as they were in I appeared from behind the door and slammed it shut.

'What—?' I could hear Wally begin to say, but too late. It only took a second to slide the bolt on the outside of the door into place, and they were well and truly trapped. Bernetta joined me, just as I was sticking a sign that read 'Out Of Order' on the door.

'Poetic justice, I think,' I grinned at Bernetta, and then we set off to see what sort of food the hotel had.

As it turned out, it was this simple act of shutting the three bullies in that toilet and sticking that 'Out Of Order' sign on the door that started all the trouble.

If you remember Herbert was on his way to the hotel reception to put the red case with the stolen statue in it into the hotel's safe.

Unfortunately for Herbert he was dying to go to the toilet, and even more unfortunately every toilet he came to had an 'Out Of Order' sign on it.

Finally he found a toilet that appeared to be in working order. He put the little red case down outside the door, and went in. But as luck would have it, this toilet was right opposite my gran's hotel room, and my gran was coming back from the restaurant with her friend Ethel when she saw the red case in the corridor.

'Good Heavens, Ethel. Look!' she said.

'What?' said Ethel.

'My red case. I could have sworn I'd taken it in. Oh well.'

And with that Gran picked up the red case and took it into her room.

● ● ● ● ● ● ● ● ● ●

16

Bonnie and Clyde were relaxing in their room, happily working out how much money they'd make from selling the statue, when Herbert came rushing back into the room flapping his arms in panic.

'It's gone!' he shouted. 'It's gone!'

Bonnie and Clyde looked at him, baffled.

'What's gone?' they asked.

'The case with the statue in.'

This made them both leap up.

'What?! How?!'

'I couldn't help it,' explained Herbert. 'I just had to go to the toilet—'

Bonnie held out her hand to shut him up.

'Don't say any more,' she said grimly. 'It's that Boyes kid!'

'He must have taken it while I was in the loo,' said Herbert.

'Now he's got it he's not going to give it up easily,' pointed out Clyde.

Bonnie thought it over.

'If there was only some lever we had against

him,' she pondered. 'Something to force him to hand it back.'

'His parents are staying here. Perhaps if we kidnapped them and refused to release them until he hands the statue over. . . ?' suggested Clyde.

Bonnie shook her head.

'No, that's no use, we've already seen how little regard he has for them. If only there was someone else.'

Herbert thought about it, and he suddenly remembered how he had seen me and Bernetta walking away from one of the toilets he tried that had an 'Out Of Order' sign on it.

'There was this little girl he was with when I saw him,' he said slowly.

Clyde clapped his hands together.

'That's it!' he said.

'What is?' asked Bonnie.

'A girlfriend!' said Clyde. 'Love, the Achilles heel of even the Greatest Man.' And here he gave Bonnie a hideous, simpering smile which was supposed to show his affection for her.

● ● ● ● ● ● ● ● ● ●

I must admit when I found out about all this afterwards I was outraged. Love! I had a good mind to sue him for libel. The idea of me and Bernetta being in love would have done my street credibility no good at all and in my opinion Clyde therefore got exactly what he deserved later on. However I'm getting ahead of myself. The outcome of this little panic-stricken meeting between the three crooks was that Bernetta suddenly vanished. We had arranged to meet by the hotel kitchen and see what fun we could get up to, ruining the dinners, but she never turned up.

This struck me as strange because Bernetta is usually very punctual, especially if there's a dodge waiting to be done. I was just standing there, pondering on this, when suddenly a hand grabbed me from behind, and I found myself pushed in a corner, and face to face with the three lunatic crooks who I'd last seen chasing me round and round my school. Here, in Boulogne! I was so astonished that I couldn't speak at first. Not that the three crooks gave me much chance to.

'We want something you've got,' said the man with the badly fitting wig. 'Something that belongs to us.'

I looked blankly back at them, bewildered. Of all places to run into this trio of lunatics! I couldn't believe it! Was there nowhere safe in the world from these three?

The woman was now talking: 'In turn, we've got something of yours. If you give us back what you've got of ours, we'll give you back what we've got of yours.'

I shook my head.

'I think you're all potty,' I said. 'There's no way that I can have anything of yours. For one thing I've only just got to France. If you don't leave me alone I shall call for the police.'

In theory this should have made them leap back in alarm and run off. In practice it didn't, and with the woman's next words I found out why.

'The name inside her jacket says Bernetta Vincent,' she said.

I goggled at her. So that was why Bernetta hadn't turned up, she'd been kidnapped by these three!

'She will be released when you give us back our statue,' said the man with the ridiculous wig.

Statue? What statue? Last time this woman had been raving about me having her formula, now they were going on about a statue. I couldn't understand it.

'I don't know what you're talking about,' I said. 'What statue?'

The three crooks exchanged looks to show that they didn't believe me, then the woman said, 'You have just two hours to work out what we're talking about. At the end of that time we expect our statue back, or else.'

Then the small man released me, and the three of them walked away.

Two hours! I had two hours to find this statue and return it to these people. What was this statue? I didn't know what it was of or how big it was. For all I knew it was about twenty feet tall. Even worse, as these people were obviously lunatics it was quite likely that the statue didn't even exist. Yet they had given me just two hours to return it to them or they would do something horrible to Bernetta, my only friend!

I wondered if I ought to go to the police, then voted against that on two counts: one, I didn't speak French and we'd possibly end up with the French police looking for a kidnapped statue;

and two, the crooks might get panicky and do something horrible to Bernetta if the police moved in. There was always the possibility of telling the Head or Wiggis, but I discounted that straight away. That pair of idiots couldn't find their shoes on their feet, let alone deal with a problem like this. No, there was only one answer, I would have to find Bernetta myself and free her.

As it turned out, things were happening on the police front. Inspector Oiseau had worked out that his list of suspects seemed quite long, what with the three crooks, Mum and Dad, and Wiggis and the Head, and he was starting to get worried that the crooks might hand the stolen statue over to one of them while he was watching the wrong person. So, he had made a decision. He had decided to arrest the three crooks while they were still in possession (so he thought) of the stolen statue and call it a day. He'd decided that recovering the statue of Sir Hector Pump and arresting three crooks and thus being declared a Hero Of All France was better than trying to arrest a whole smuggling ring and maybe missing out and thereby becoming an Idiot Of All France.

'We know the stolen statue is in the little red case,' he said to Gaston. 'So, what do we do? We wait until we see them carrying this red case, and then we arrest them red-handed!'

What he didn't know, however, was that the three crooks had lost their red case to my Gran and were now hunting for it high and low throughout the hotel. I think they might have even started to believe that perhaps I didn't know where their red case was, because they were now exploring the possibility that someone else might have taken it. And the more they thought about it, the more their list of possible suspects narrowed down to two:

'Perhaps it was his parents who took it?' said Bonnie. 'I'm sure they were mixed up in that last business with the formula. Or, at least, his mother was.'

'You could be right,' agreed Clyde thoughtfully. 'But how do we find out?'

'There's only one way to find out,' said Bonnie. 'We look in their room.'

So it was that the three crooks checked the hotel keys to make sure that Mum and Dad were out, and then Bonnie and Herbert kept watch while Clyde sneaked into my parent's hotel room. He came out a few seconds later with Mum's red case.

'It was there?' he crowed delightedly. 'We were right!'

'*I* was right,' Bonnie corrected him. 'Okay, let's get it to the hotel's safe before anything else happens to it.'

And with that they rushed off along the corridor, turned a corner, and ran straight into the arms of Inspector Oiseau and Gaston.

The next bit is taken from the evidence that was presented when the whole thing came out in court some months later, and led the French newspapers to call poor Inspector Oiseau

'Inspector Idiot'. Personally I think they were a bit unfair on him. After all, how was he to know that there were four identical red suitcases all circulating in the hotel at the same time.

For the moment he was feeling pretty proud as he paced up and down his office, looking at the glum faces of Bonnie, Clyde and Herbert who were sitting on three chairs and guarded by Gaston.

'You thought when you stole that statue that you were dealing with *les imbeciles*,' he said. 'Well, let me inform you that little did you know that you were up against none other than Inspector Oiseau of the Sûreté.'

Bonnie, Clyde and Herbert said nothing. The Inspector tapped the little red case on the desk in front of him.

'*Madame et messieurs*,' he said, 'I have reason to believe that when I open this red case I will find a statue of Sir Hector Pump which has been stolen from the Musée de la Pump in Toulouse. *Et Voilà!*'

And with that he opened the case . . . and pulled out my Mum's nightdress. The crooks looked at the contents of the case, baffled. Bonnie recovered first, kicked Herbert to stop him saying anything to give them away, and then said acidly: 'Does that look like a statue, Inspector?'

Bewildered, the Inspector looked at the name tag inside the case.

'Mrs Susan Boyes,' he read, 'Winterton Drive . . .'

'Exactly,' said Bonnie. 'I am Susan Boyes and that is my case with my personal belongings.'

183

'I assume that we may now leave, Inspector, and that a written apology will be forthcoming?' said Clyde, just to rub salt in the wound.

Helplessly the Inspector handed over the red case to Bonnie, and then watched as the three crooks swept out of the office. As soon as they were gone he turned on Gaston.

'Imbecile! You said the statue was inside a small red case!' he raged.

'It was, *m'sieur l'inspecteur*,' protested Gaston. 'I don't understand it.'

Suddenly realization dawned in the Inspector's brain.

'Of course!' he said. 'The old red case switch! There is another red case containing the statue which they have passed on to their accomplice. Come, Gaston! Let us return to the hotel immediately! We shall now catch the real smuggler!'

17

Meanwhile I was searching the hotel from top to bottom looking for Bernetta, but with no luck whatsoever. I decided there was only one answer and that was to follow the crooks. Sooner or later they would have to go and check on Bernetta in case she had got away. All I had to do was wait and watch and let them lead me to her.

I went down to the hotel reception to try and find out what their room number was, and just as I was entering the lobby the three crooks came in through the door, the man with the ill-fitting wig carrying a small red case. They were talking amongst themselves, obviously very worried over something, and I heard the woman say, 'But if this isn't our case, then where is it?'

Just at that moment Wiggis appeared, also carrying a small red case, this one containing all our school work sheets for the French trip. He went up to the reception desk, put his case down, and went behind the desk looking for something. The crook with the badly-fitting wig lost no time at all, he rushed over to Wiggis's case, picked it up, then put his red case in its place, and then hurried back to his two accomplices.

Wiggis came back from behind the desk, not having found whatever it was he was looking for, and picked up what he thought was his red case, just as the door of the hotel opened and the Inspector and Gaston the gendarme entered. They took one look at Wiggis, standing there holding the red case, and then the Inspector said: 'Gaston! Arrest that man!'

'What?' squawked Wiggis, but before he could say another word he was grabbed by the two policemen and hustled out into a waiting police car.

Although I would have liked to have known what it was all about and why Wiggis was being arrested, I had more important things to do, namely to find Bernetta. I watched as the three crooks hurried off, carrying Wiggis's case, and then went after them at a discreet distance.

The first thing the three crooks did was hurry to their room to check the contents of Wiggis's case. The second thing they did was howl and moan and groan after they'd opened it and found all these school work sheets, a similar reaction to our class when we get work sheets from Wiggis.

'This isn't the statue!' said Clyde.

'I'm convinced it's that Bryan Boyes who's behind this!' snapped Bonnie. 'And I think it's time to put some pressure on him.'

'How?' said Herbert.

'We use the girl,' said Bonnie evilly.

I hid behind a cupboard in the corridor and watched them come out of their room, and then set off for the stairs. They were on their way to

Bernetta! Making sure that I wasn't seen, I followed them.

They went up to the very top of these really dusty old stairs, to a part of the hotel that I hadn't spotted. They went through a door and on to this dingy, grey corridor which must have been right underneath the roof. They opened another door, and went in. I could just see Bernetta tied and gagged, sitting on a chair.

Bonnie went over to Bernetta and slipped the gag down from her mouth.

'Right, my little beauty,' she said, menacingly, 'it's time for you to do something useful. You're going to tell your little boyfriend to give us back the statue.'

'He's not my boyfriend and I don't know what you're talking about,' said Bernetta.

'Oh no?' said Bonnie evilly. 'Herbert.'

'Yes?' said Herbert.

'Show her what we mean,' snarled Bonnie.

'Right,' said Herbert, and he held his hands about eighteen inches apart. 'The statue is about this big—'

'Not the statue, you idiot!' howled Bonnie. 'Show her we mean business.'

Clyde looked shocked.

'Bonnie, you don't mean——!' he began.

'Oh yes I do,' she snarled.

I decided it was time to act. After all, Bernetta is my best and only friend.

'Oh no you don't!' I yelled, and I threw myself at Herbert, trying to wrestle him to the ground.

Have you noticed how this always works in films? The hero comes upon a cave or a castle or something where the captives are held, and there are about two hundred villains, all armed to the teeth, and the hero appears and with two punches knocks them all over. Well I've got news for you, in real life it doesn't work like that. In this case I managed to get one punch in on Herbert and all I did was hurt my hand.

Five minutes later I, too, was tied and gagged and sitting on a chair next to Bernetta.

'What shall we do with him?' asked Clyde. 'Shall we make him tell us where it is?'

Bonnie shook her head.

'It'll take too long,' she said. 'We want to be on that ferry tomorrow with the statue. We'll lock him in here with her, then we'll look for it. He can only have hidden it in this hotel.'

And with that all three went out, leaving Bernetta and me trapped in that dusty old attic. We were doomed!

Mind you, if I thought I was doomed, Inspector Oiseau of the Sûreté was beginning to think that he was not far from being doomed himself. He had had to let Wiggis go after finding that his case was once again the one with Mum's nightdress in, although he had cautioned Wiggis as a possible bag-snatcher and told him that if he found him with anyone else's case he would arrest him on the spot and throw him in jail for hundreds of years.

While Bernetta and I were locked up and tied up in the attic at the top of the hotel, the Inspector and Gaston were just returning,

determined to find the real red case with the stolen statue in it.

'I am beginning to think there is a conspiracy against me in this case,' stormed the Inspector.

'Which case?' asked Gaston, unsure as to which case he was talking about. 'The little red case?'

'The case of the stolen statue,' clarified the Inspector. 'I am fed up with the little red cases! The red cases is a red herring!'

Gaston frowned, puzzled.

'How can a case be a herring?' he asked.

'It is a ploy to throw me off the scent,' the Inspector declaimed.

Just at that moment who should enter the hotel lobby but my gran and her friend Ethel, Gran carrying her red case with all her emergency supplies of food in it. Gaston saw it and at once tapped the Inspector on the arm.

'M'sieur l'Inspecteur!' he said urgently, and he pointed to the red case in my gran's hand.

The Inspector looked, then shook his head, resisting. '*Non,*' he said. 'It is a red herring!'

'But say it is the correct case?' said Gaston.

The Inspector hesitated, then he moved towards my gran and Ethel.

'*Mesdames!*' he said. '*Attendez!*'

And that was how my gran and Ethel were arrested and ended up in a French police station.

What about the other red cases, you ask yourself? Particularly, where was the one with the stolen statue in it?

If you remember, my gran had started all this trouble by taking it into her room, thinking it was *her* red case. Once she found her own case was already inside her room, however, she realized she'd made a mistake. Because it looked the same as hers she thought it might be my mum's, so she went along to my mum and dad's room in the hotel and asked if my mum had lost her case. As it happened Mum had, because Clyde had just taken it. So it was that Gran handed Mum the case with the stolen statue in, and Mum put it down beside the dressing table. If only one of them had bothered to open the case the whole problem would have then been sorted out much earlier, but that's the trouble with my family – you just can't trust them to do anything right.

However, what had happened to our hero (me) and Bernetta? (I hope you are asking.) The answer is, we had managed to break out. All those years of watching thriller films on television had finally paid off, because we pushed our chairs back to back, and then I was able to untie the ropes that held Bernetta. Once she was undone she was able to untie me, and we were free!

After that it was plain sailing. The fact that the three crooks had locked the door when they left us in the attic room turned out to be no problem, because I found a screwdriver in the corner of the room. It was a simple matter to unscrew the lock on the door, and then we were out.

The rest of the people in the hotel were also

having a difficult time of it, though in their own different ways.

Wiggis was still fuming over the fact that he'd been arrested. He'd also noticed that a few of his pupils were missing.

'I tell you, Headmaster,' he said. 'there is something funny going on in this hotel.'

'Oh, surely not,' said the Head in his usual wishy-washy way.

'No?' queried Wiggis. 'I have searched this place high and low, yet there is still no sign of either Bryan Boyes or Bernetta Vincent.'

'Are you sure?' asked the Head.

Wiggis nodded.

'Nor Edward Slogg,' he added. 'Nor Walters, nor Juggins.'

'Oh dear,' said the Head unhappily.

'Add to that the fact that my case with the French trip work sheets has disappeared, *and* that I was arrested as a suspected bag-snatcher—'

'I'm sure there is a perfectly reasonable explanation for all of this,' said the Head, trying to pacify Wiggis.

'Of course there is,' said Wiggis vengefully. 'Bryan Boyes.'

'I do think you're being a bit hard on him,' said the Head.

'I would be if I could find him,' snorted Wiggis. 'No, perhaps there is something up. Something that is even bigger than Bryan Boyes.'

'What?' asked the Head.

'That is what I intend to find out,' said Wiggis. 'I am going to see the British Consul.'

This shocked the Head, who hated upsetting authority of any sort whatsoever.

'The British Consul?' he said, horrified. 'Are you sure that's necessary?'

'With five children and my suitcase missing, and the police arresting me?' said Wiggis. 'It is vital!'

Meanwhile, what had happened to Wally, Slug and Juggs? Unlike me and Bernetta they weren't lucky enough to find a screwdriver to get them out of their tight corner. They had spent all this time pushing against the toilet door, trying to break the bolt that held it, and finally they had succeeded. One last bash, the door finally came off its hinges, and the three of them tumbled out into the corridor.

'Right, Bryan Boyes!' snarled Wally. 'You've gone too far this time!'

And the three of them picked themselves up and set off to search the hotel to find me and tear me limb from limb.

During all this the poor Inspector was dragging himself back to the hotel, fed up with the English, fed up with Sir Hector Pump, and fed up with red cases. He had had a real roasting from my gran for arresting her. I think she'd actually gone as far as hitting him with her umbrella before he'd released her. Whatever had happened, it had finally made him lose his temper with Gaston who he blamed for this fiasco, claiming that if Gaston hadn't mentioned the red case to him none of this would ever have happened. Gaston had replied that, in his opinion, the Inspector couldn't find the Eiffel Tower in the middle of Paris. In return the Inspector, losing his temper, had punched Gaston in the eye. This was the last straw as far as Gaston was concerned, and when they arrived back at the hotel to continue their search for the elusive stolen statue of Sir Hector Pump, they weren't talking. Well, the Inspector was, and so was Gaston, but not in a friendly fashion.

'I shall complain to the Authorities,' said Gaston primly, rubbing his eye. 'It is police brutality.'

'I have already said, Gaston, that I apologize,' said the Inspector for the umpteenth time. 'I do not know what came over me. It is all the fault of these English!'

'I want to be taken off this case,' insisted Gaston, not mollified.

'But the case is nearly solved, believe me!' pleaded the Inspector.

'I still want to be taken off it,' repeated Gaston firmly. 'I have only one eye left.'

'Trust me, Gaston,' implored the Inspector. 'We know the statue is not in this red case. It is therefore in one of the other red cases. So, I shall open every red case in this hotel and that way we will find the stolen statue!'

'I still want to be taken off this case,' repeated Gaston stubbornly.

By now they had arrived at the hotel. They walked into the lobby, and the first person they saw was Wiggis, on his way to the British Consul, with the Head hanging on to his arm in an effort to stop him from creating a scandal which would reflect badly on the school.

'Ah-ha, the bag snatcher and his assistant!' whispered the Inspector urgently to Gaston. 'Soon the case will be solved!'

'I still wish to be taken off this case,' said Gaston firmly.

The Inspector stood in front of Wiggis and the Head.

'*Messieurs*!' he commanded. '*Halte*!'

'I beg your pardon?' said the Head, bewildered.

'It's those idiotic policemen who arrested me,' said Wiggis.

The Head looked worried, having visions of our school's reputation disappearing down the pan as soon as news of this leaked out.

'The police!' he said. 'Oh dear!'

Just at that moment, in walked Bonnie, Clyde and Herbert, carrying Wiggis's red case. They spotted the Inspector and were just about to sneak off, when the Inspector saw them.

'*Attendez*!' he called out, and they stopped. 'Gaston, take that case!'

Gaston sniffed, but went to the crooks and took the red case from them. He was just doing this when Mum and Dad walked into the lobby, Mum carrying the red case with the stolen statue in it.

'Really,' she was complaining, 'it is all too bad—'

She stopped when she saw everyone standing around as if they were in a play.

'Is something the matter?' she asked.

'Yes, madame,' said the Inspector. 'I will trouble you to give me your red case.'

'This?' said Mum. 'It isn't mine. Mine's got all my nightclothes in. All this has got in it is this.'

And she opened the case and took out the missing statue of Sir Hector Pump. That was it, chaos and confusion! Herbert started to say, 'It's ours,' but Bonnie stuck her hand over his mouth. The Inspector and Gaston each started shouting at each other. Wally and Juggs and Slug appeared, still intent on finding me and doing me harm, but curious to see what all this noise was about. The only one who seemed pleased about the whole thing was Wiggis, who smirked at the Inspector and said: 'See? The proof that I am innocent!'

However the Inspector had had Wiggis marked down as a suspicious character from the start and he wasn't going to let him off that easily.

'*Non!*' he said. 'You I know to be the notorious bag-snatcher. I suspect you have a hand in this somewhere, so I also arrest you!'

Wiggis gaped at him.

'What?' he yelled, shocked.

Wally and Slug decided it was time to come to Wiggis's aid.

'You can't arrest him!' protested Wally.

'No,' chimed in Slug. 'He's our teacher.'

This was all the Inspector needed to complete his case.

'As I suspected!' he announced triumphantly. 'You are the Oliver Nickleby Fagin! You teach these *pauvre enfants les* crookery. I arrest you! In fact, I arrest everyone in this hotel!'

And with that he pulled out a police whistle,

gave a long blast on it, and then whole hotel erupted into chaos.

Bernetta and I, of course, knew nothing about any of this. We had managed to get out of the attic room and had gone down to the lobby to find someone to report the three crooks to, but there was no one there. In fact, by the time we got down, there was absolutely no one at all in the whole hotel! It was like one of those science-fiction films where creatures from Outer Space turn up and kidnap a whole townload of people. It was weird.

'There's absolutely no one here at all!' said Bernetta after we'd searched the whole hotel at least three times. 'Even the staff have gone.'

'I know,' I said. 'Odd, isn't it?'

'What are we going to do?' she asked.

'There's only one thing we can do,' I said. 'We'd better go and tell the police there's something funny going on here.'

Which is how I came to be the hero of the hour.

The Inspector had taken no chances. Convinced that all the people in the hotel were involved in some huge conspiracy over the smuggling of the statue of Sir Hector Pump into England, he had arrested absolutely everybody, including the local postman who'd only called in to deliver a letter. Consequently the local jail was full to busting, with Mum and Dad, Gran and Ethel, Wiggis and the Head, Bonnie, Clyde, Herbert, Wally, Slug, Juggs, all our school party and

Uncle Tom Cobbley and all — everyone under lock and key and shouting furiously, protesting their innocence, while the Inspector shouted at them all to shut up.

'It's Bryan Boyes who's behind this!' shouted Wiggis, determined to blame me for everything.

'What do you mean?' demanded Mum indignantly.

'I'm sorry, Mrs Boyes,' said Wiggis, not sorry at all, 'but facts are facts. Your son is at the root of nearly everything that's ever happened involving this school!'

'That's not fair!' said Dad.

'Quite right,' agreed Mum.

'It was Bryan Boyes who locked us in the toilet,' pointed out The Slug.

'Who is this Bryan Boyes?' asked the Inspector, puzzled at this new name coming into the jigsaw.

'Although I do sympathize, Mrs Boyes,' continued Wiggis, ignoring the Inspector and warming to his theme of blaming me; 'it is a fact that your Bryan does seem to have an unfortunate habit of being wherever there is trouble.'

'Well not in this case!' defended Mum.

'Oh yes he is!' accused Wally.

'Oh no he isn't,' said Mum and Dad.

'Oh yes he is!' shouted everybody else in the cells, and they proceeded to set up a chant: 'Bryan Boyes! Bryan Boyes! Bryan Boyes!'

'Shut up!!!!' screamed the Inspector, and everybody shut up.

'I ask you again, who is this Bryan Boyes?' demanded the Inspector, and it was at that moment that Bernetta and I walked into the police station and saw everyone stuffed behind bars.

'Did I hear my name?' I asked.

That did it. Immediately there was an outcry from everybody, most of them shouting at me accusingly. Above it all I could hear Dad calling, 'Are you alright, son?'

'Silence!' roared the Inspector, and everyone shut up. 'Right Bryan Boyes,' he said, turning to me, 'What is going on here? And who are all these people?'

One by one I started to tell him who everybody was.

'That's my mum and dad,' I said. 'That's my gran. That's my teacher. That's my headmaster. Those are three rotten bullies who tried to lock me in a toilet.'

'No we didn't!' shouted Juggs and Slug, and they turned on Wally. 'It's all your fault!'

The Inspector pointed at the three lunatics who'd locked me and Bernetta up.

'And who are these three?' he asked.

I shook my head. 'I don't know,' I said, 'except they're the ones who kidnapped us and tied us up and kept going on about wanting their statue back, or else.'

'They're crooks!' said Bernetta firmly.

The Inspector beamed happily.

'*Bon!*' he said. 'Gaston, release everyone except those three crooks!'

And with that Gaston the gendarme began to open the cell doors and everyone stumbled out, delighted at being free at last.

'And for this,' the Inspector reminded them, 'you have this boy to thank: this Bryan Boyes.'

'Three cheers for Bryan!' said Dad. 'Hip hip . . .'

'Hooray!'

And with that they all trooped off, all except for the three crooks who were now well and truly behind bars. Bernetta and I grinned at each other. Then a thought suddenly struck me.

'Hey, hang on a minute!' I said.

'What?' asked Bernetta.

'They forgot to give me my other two cheers.'

More Beaver Books

On the following pages you will find some other exciting Beaver Books to look out for in your local bookshop

BEAVER BOOKS FOR OLDER READERS

There are loads of exciting books for older readers in Beaver. They are available in bookshops or they can be ordered directly from us. Just complete the form below and send the right money and the books will be sent to you at home.

☐ WATER LANE	Tom Aitken	£1.95
☐ FRANKENSTEIN	David Campton	£1.75
☐ IN THE GRIP OF WINTER	Colin Dann	£1.99
☐ TWISTED CIRCUITS	Mick Gowar	£1.75
☐ FANGS OF THE WEREWOLF	John Halkin	£1.95
☐ TEMPEST TWINS Books 1 – 4	John Harvey	£1.99
☐ YOUR FRIEND, REBECCA	Linda Hoy	£1.99
☐ REDWALL	Brian Jacques	£2.95
☐ THE GOOSEBERRY	Joan Lingard	£1.95
☐ WHITE FANG	Jack London	£1.95
☐ ALANNA	Tamora Pearce	£2.50
☐ A SHIVER OF FEAR	Emlyn Roberts	£1.95
☐ A BOTTLED CHERRY ANGEL	Jean Ure	£1.99
☐ THE MAGICIANS OF CAPRONA	Daina Wynne-Jones	£1.95

If you would like to order books, please send this form, and the money due to:
ARROW BOOKS, BOOKSERVICE BY POST, PO BOX 29, DOUGLAS, ISLE OF MAN, BRITISH ISLES. Please enclose a cheque or postal order made out to Arrow Books Ltd for the amount due including 22p per book for postage and packing both for orders within the UK and for overseas orders.

NAME . . . .

ADDRESS . . . .

. . . .

Please print clearly.